CHRISTMAS
IN THE
ADIRONDACKS.

ADIRONDACK MURRAY'S
CONTRIBUTION TO
"Ye Joyous Season."

How John Norton, the Trapper, Kept His Christmas,
and
John Norton's Vagabond.

The reception which the American public have given to these two celebrated stories, places them in the first rank of English Composition. For the first time they are now published in HOLIDAY EDITION FORM. It is the AUTHOR'S AUTOGRAPH EDITION, and strictly limited. It contains a lifelike portrait of Mr. Murray, and a quotation on the autograph leaf from his writings in his own hand, thus not only introducing to lovers of unique book lore a volume which stands apart in its quaint and lovable mingling of humor, pathos and dramatic incident, but one that will rank with those treasured works that stamp themselves with a special value as time goes on and the difficulty of obtaining a copy increases.

This volume, as is true also in reference to all others of Mr. Murray's enlarged and revised works, can be obtained from the author directly, or from some authorized agent.

Subscriptions (for one week) received here. Subscriber can pay and take the book along with him, or have it sent (C. O. D.) to any part of the city.

Parties wishing to send them to distant friends as Christmas gifts, can have them so sent promptly upon their ordering, at OUR EXPENSE.

Only a Limited Number of Volumes Left.
BUY NOW.

Introduction

Who exactly was John Norton? Drawing upon the manuscripts, scrapbooks of press clippings and memorabilia of author, William H. H. ("Adirondack") Murray, recently given to the Adirondack Museum, his story can now be told.

"I never saw any such man as John Norton," wrote Murray, "never saw one as good as he is, in my vision of him, never saw one that even suggested him. He is a creation, pure and simple, of my imagination. He nevertheless stands for an actual type. Big-bodied, big-headed, big-hearted, wise, humorous, humane and brave, he typifies to me the old-fashioned New England man who, having lived his life in the woods, has developed in him those virtues and qualities of head and heart, of mind and soul, in harmony with his life-long surroundings."

The publishing of Murray's work of 1869 had dramatic effects upon the career of the surprised author, a young Boston clergyman who originally never intended to become a national literary figure.

The book of Adirondack adventures created such a sensation that Murray was virtually compelled to move from his pulpit to public lectures—the Lyceum platform it was then called—to describe in person the real benefits to body and soul of life in the woods.

Murray shifted his ambitions to become a writer who could make his readers laugh and cry without involving a romantic element. With the Adirondacks as a background, the result was two volumes of John Norton stories. *Holiday Tales* was composed somewhat later, and was the only one which again unexpectedly brought Murray before American audiences on public speaking tours.

"How did I come to write this story?" said Murray in response to a reporter's question. "I was near the headwaters of the Ottawa River when there came over me the fever to write. So I wrote this story, and the pleasantest thing I remember about its writing was that for the first time in my life I had all the time I wanted for writing. I took a month for it." Some time later it was published as a special Christmas supplement to *Harper's Weekly* for December 22, 1883.

"How did I come to read it?" he continued. It was something of an accident two years later while visiting in Burlington, when he was asked to read something and this was the only thing he had at hand. "After that I read it forty-seven nights in succession, and after that with a break of only a night or two here or there. I kept on reading it till I had read it 172 nights in all, not because I wanted to but because it took the people's fancy and they insisted on hearing it." In the following decade he gave over five hundred readings of this same story in auditoriums and opera houses in New England and eastern Canada, at a fee of $100 to $250 an evening. The tale was published as a booklet, and was sold at the door; he was happy to autograph copies for those who asked.

Murray's success was due partly to his skills as a public speaker. "He stands before the audience a commanding figure," wrote one reporter, "over six feet in height, with a face of striking power and refinement, a manner of perfect poise and ease, and a voice of large compass and delicious tone. He speaks with a grace, a simplicity and a mastery of himself and his subject that wins instant interest, and the interest deepens the longer he speaks."

"What Dickens did for England in his immortal *Christmas Carol*, Murray has done for America," was the verdict of many critics at the time. If Murray were here today, he would probably suggest that before making up your own mind you gather a few family or friends around the living room fire, turn off the television, and read this story aloud for yourselves.

Warder H. Cadbury
Joel S. Cadbury
Indian Lake, New York

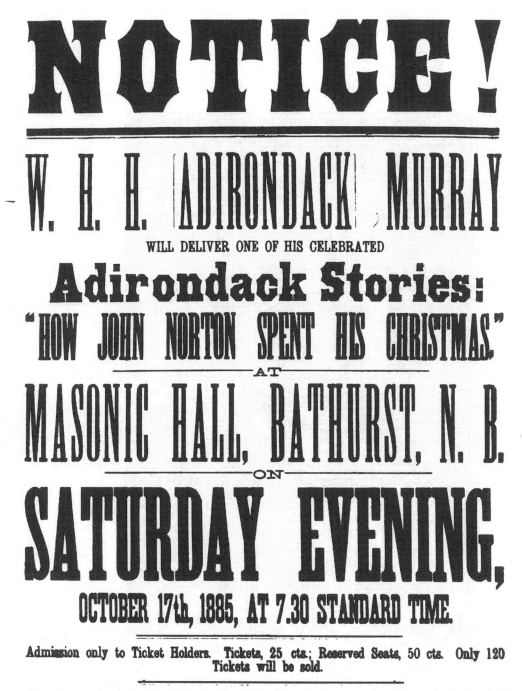

NOTICE!

W. H. H. [ADIRONDACK] MURRAY

WILL DELIVER ONE OF HIS CELEBRATED

Adirondack Stories:
"HOW JOHN NORTON SPENT HIS CHRISTMAS."

AT

MASONIC HALL, BATHURST, N. B.

ON

SATURDAY EVENING,

OCTOBER 17th, 1885, AT 7.30 STANDARD TIME.

Admission only to Ticket Holders. Tickets, 25 cts.; Reserved Seats, 50 cts. Only 120 Tickets will be sold.

In this recitation of one of his Celebrated Adirondack Tales, which have given him his literary name and fame, Mr. Murray stands revealed to his audience in his best light as author and orator. The tenderness of the sentiment, the keen wit, the quiet humor and the sweet pathos of this story are peculiarly his own. No one but Murray could have written "John Norton's Christmas," and no one but Murray could tell it as he does.

Tickets can be had at the Stores of K. F. Burns & Co., R. A. & J. Stewart, and from John Sivewright.

Courier Job Print, Bathurst.

W. H. H. MURRAY,
THE MURRAY HOMESTEAD, GUILFORD, CONN.

Oh. Memory. Thou

Treasure dear that

lingeth on forever!

W. P. P. Murray

Dec 25 - 1898

CHRISTMAS IN THE ADIRONDACKS

W. H. H. Murray

BOOKS
NORTH COUNTRY BOOKS

Essex, Connecticut

BOOKS
NORTH COUNTRY BOOKS

An imprint of Globe Pequot, the trade division of
The Rowman & Littlefield Publishing Group, Inc.
4501 Forbes Blvd., Ste. 200
Lanham, MD 20706
www.rowman.com

Distributed by NATIONAL BOOK NETWORK

Introduction text Copyright © 1995 by North Country Books, Inc. Broadsides are Courtesy of
The Adirondack Museum.

British Library Cataloguing in Publication Information available

Library of Congress Cataloging-in-Publication Data Available

ISBN 9781493077458 (paper : alk. paper) | ISBN 9781493077465 (ebook)

♾™ The paper used in this publication meets the minimum requirements of American National
Standard for Information Sciences—Permanence of Paper for Printed Library Materials,
ANSI/NISO Z39.48-1992.

CONTENTS.

I.

THE WILD DEER'S HOME.

THE OLD TRAPPER'S HOME.

LIST OF ILLUSTRATIONS

    "Friends come and go, but until death enters kennel or cabin the hunter and his hounds
        bide together."

HOW JOHN NORTON THE TRAPPER KEPT HIS CHRISTMAS.

I.

A CABIN. A cabin in the woods. In the cabin a great fire-place piled high with logs, fiercely ablaze. On either side of the broad hearthstone a hound sat on his haunches, looking gravely, as only a hound in a meditative mood can, into the glowing fire. In the center of the cabin, whose every nook and corner was bright with the ruddy firelight, stood a wooden table, strongly built and solid. At the table sat John Norton, poring over a book, — a book large of size, with wooden covers bound in leather, brown with age, and smooth as with the handling of many generations. The whitened head of the old man was bowed over the broad page, on which one hand rested, with the forefinger marking the sentence. A cabin in the woods filled with firelight, a table, a book, an old man studying the book. This was the scene on Christmas Eve. Outside, the earth was white with snow, and in the blue sky above the snow was the white moon.

"It says here," said the Trapper, speaking to himself, "it says here, ' *Give to him that lacketh, and from him that hath not, withhold not thine hand.*' It be a good sayin' fur sartin ; and the world would be a good deal better off, as I conceit, ef the folks follered the sayin' a leetle more closely." And here the old man paused a moment, and, with his hand still resting on the page, and his forefinger still pointing at the sentence, seemed pondering what he had been reading. At last he broke the silence again, saying : —

"Yis, the world would be a good deal better off, ef the folks in it follered the sayin';" and then he added, "There's another spot in the book I'd orter look at to-night; it's a good ways furder on, but I guess I can find it. Henry says the furder on you git in the book, the better it grows, and I conceit the boy may be right; for there be a good deal of murderin' and fightin' in the fore part of the book, that don't make pleasant readin', and what the Lord wanted to put it in fur is a good deal more than a man without book-larnin' can understand. Murderin' be murderin', whether it be in the Bible or out of the Bible ; and puttin' it in the Bible, and sayin' it was done by the Lord's commandment, don't make it any better. And a good deal of the fightin' they did in the old time was sartinly without reason and ag'in jedgment, specially where they killed the women-folks and the leetle uns." And while the old man had thus been communicating with himself, touching the character of the Old Testament, he had been turning the leaves until he had reached the opening chapters of the New, and had come to the description of the Saviour's birth, and the angelic announcement of it on the earth. Here he paused, and began to read. He read as an old man unaccustomed to letters must read, — slowly and

THE OLD TRAPPER'S FIREPLACE.

with a show of labor, but with perfect contentment as to his progress, and a brightening face.

"This isn't a trail a man can hurry on onless he spends a good deal of his time on it, or is careless about notin' the signs, fur the words be weighty, and a man must stop at each word, and look around awhile, in order to git all the meanin' out of 'em — yis, a man orter travel this trail a leetle slow, ef he wants to see all there is to see on it."

Then the old man began to read : —

" ' *Then there was with the angels a multitude of the heavenly host,*' — the exact number isn't sot down here," he muttered ; "but I conceit there may have been three or four hunderd, — '*praisin' God and singin', Glory to God in the highest, and on 'arth, peace to men of good will.*' That's right," said the Trapper. "Yis, peace to men of good will. That be the sort that desarve peace ; the other kind orter stand their chances." And here the old man closed the book, — closed it slowly, and with the care we take of a treasured thing ; closed it, fastened the clasps, and carried it to the great chest whence he had taken it, putting it away in its place. Having done this, he returned to his seat, and, moving the chair in front of the fire, he looked first at one hound, and then at the other, and said, "Pups, this be Christmas Eve, and I sartinly trust ye be grateful fur the comforts ye have."

He said this deliberately, as if addressing human companions. The two hounds turned their heads toward their master, looked placidly into his face, and wagged their tails.

"Yis, yis, I understand ye," said the Trapper. "Ye both be comfortable, and, I dare say, that arter yer way ye both be grateful, fur, next to eatin', a dog loves the heat, and ye be nigh enough to the logs to be toastin'. Yis, this be Christmas Eve," continued the old man, "and in the settlements the folks be gittin' ready their gifts. The young people be tyin' up the evergreens, and the leetle uns be onable to sleep because of their dreamin'. It's a pleasant pictur', and I sartinly wish I could see the merry-makin's, as Henry has told me of them, sometime, but I trust it may be in his own house, and with his own children." With this pleasant remark, in respect to the one he loved so well, the old man lapsed into silence. But the peaceful contentment of his face, as the firelight revealed it, showed plainly that, though his lips moved not, his mind was still active with pleasant thoughts of the one whose name he had mentioned, and whom he so fondly loved. At last a more sober look came to his countenance,— a look of regret, of self-reproach, the look of a man who remembers something he should not have forgotten,—and he said :—

"I ax the Lord to pardin me, that in the midst of my plenty I have forgot them that may be in want. The shanty sartinly looked open enough the last time I fetched the trail past the clearin', and though with the help of the moss and the clay in the bank she might make it comfortable, yit, ef the vagabond that be her husband has forgot his own, and desarted them, as Wild Bill said he had, I doubt ef there be vict'als enough in the shanty to keep them from starvin'. Yis, pups," said the old man, rising, "it'll be a good tramp through the snow, but we'll go in the mornin', and see ef the woman be in want. The boy himself said, when he stopped at the shanty last summer, afore he went out, that he didn't see how they was to git through the winter, and I reckon he left the woman some money, by the way she follered him toward the boat; and he told me to bear them in mind when the snow came, and see to it they didn't suffer. I might as well git the pack-basket out, and begin to put the things in't, fur it be a goodly distance, and an 'arly start will make the day pleasant to the woman and the leetle uns, ef vict'als be scant in the cupboard. Yis, I'll git the pack-basket out, and look round a leetle, and see what I can find to take 'em. I don't conceit it'll make much of a show, fur what might be good fur a man won't be of sarvice to a woman; and as fur the leetle uns, I don't know ef I've got a single thing but vict'als that'll fit 'em. Lord! ef I was near the settlements, I might swap a dozen skins fur jest what I wanted to give 'em; but I'll git the basket out, and look round and see what I've got."

In a moment the great pack-basket had been placed in the middle of the floor, and the Trapper was busy overhauling his stores to see what he could find that would make a fitting Christmas gift for those he was to visit on the morrow. A canister of tea was first deposited on the table, and, after he had smelled of it, and placed a few grains of it on his tongue, like a connoisseur, he proceeded to pour more than half of its contents into a little bark box, and, having carefully tied the cover, he placed it in the basket.

"The yarb be of the best," said the old man, putting his nose to the mouth of the canister, and taking a long sniff before he inserted the stopple — "the yarb be of the best, fur the smell of it goes into the nose strong as mustard. That be good fur the woman fur sartin, and will cheer her sperits when she be downhearted; fur a woman takes as naterally to tea as an otter to his slide, and I warrant it'll be an amazin' comfort to her, arter the day's work be over, more specially ef the work had been heavy, and gone sorter crosswise. Yis, the yarb be good fur a woman when things go crosswise, and the box'll be a great help to her many and many a night, beyend doubt. The Lord sartinly had women in mind when He made the yarb, and a kindly feelin' fur their infarmities, and, I dare say, they be grateful accordin' to their knowledge."

A large cake of maple sugar followed the tea into the basket, and a small chest of honey accompanied it.

"That's honest sweetenin'," remarked the Trapper with decided emphasis; "and that is more'n ye can say of the sugar of the settlements, leastwise ef a man can jedge by the stuff they peddle at the clearin'. The bees be no cheats; and a man who taps his own trees, and biles the runnin' into sugar under his own eye, knows what kind of sweetenin' he's gittin'. The woman won't find any sand in her teeth when she takes a bite from that loaf, or stirs a leetle of the honey in the cup she's steepin'."

Some salt and pepper were next added to the packages already in the basket. A sack of flour and another of Indian meal followed. A generous round of pork, and a bag of jerked venison, that would balance a twenty-pound weight, at least, went into the pack. On these, several large-sized salmon trout, that had been smoked by the Trapper's best skill, were laid. These offerings evidently exhausted the old man's resources, for, after looking round a while, and searching the cupboard from bottom to top, he returned to the basket, and contemplated it with satisfaction, indeed, yet with a face slightly shaded with disappointment.

"The vict'als be all right," he said, "fur there be enough to last 'em a month, and they needn't scrimp themselves either. But eatin' isn't all, and the leetle uns was nigh on to naked the last time I seed 'em; and the woman's dress, in spite of the patchin', looked as ef it would desart her, ef she didn't keep a close eye on't. Lord! Lord! what shall I do? fur there's room enough in the basket, and the woman and the leetle uns need garments; that is, it's more'n likely they do, and I haven't a garment in the cabin to take 'em."

"Hillo! Hillo! John Norton! John Norton! Hillo!" The voice came sharp and clear, cutting keenly through the frosty air and the cabin walls. "John Norton!"

"Wild Bill!" exclaimed the Trapper. "I sartinly hope the vagabond hasn't been a-drinkin'. His voice sounds as ef he was sober; but the chances be ag'in the signs, fur, ef he isn't drunk, the marcy of the Lord or the scarcity of liquor has kept him from it. I'll go to the door, and see what he wants. It's sartinly too cold to let a man stand in the holler long, whether

2

he be sober or drunk;" with which remark the Trapper stepped to the door, and flung it open.

"What is it, Wild Bill? what is it?" he called. "Be ye drunk, or be ye sober, that ye stand there shoutin' in the cold with a log cabin within a dozen rods of ye?"

"Sober, John Norton, sober. Sober as a Moravian preacher at a funeral."

"Yer trappin' must have been mighty poor, then, Wild Bill, for the last month, or the Dutchman at the clearin' has watered his liquor by a wrong measure for once. But ef ye be sober, why do ye stand there whoopin' like an Indian, when the ambushment is onkivered and the bushes be alive with the knaves? Why don't ye come into the cabin, like a sensible man, ef ye be sober? The signs be ag'in ye, Wild Bill; yis, the signs be ag'in ye."

"Come into the cabin!" retorted Bill. "An' so I would mighty lively, ef I could; but the load is heavy, and your path is as slippery as the plank over the creek at the Dutchman's, when I've two horns aboard."

"Load! What load have ye been draggin' through the woods?" exclaimed the Trapper. "Ye talk as ef my cabin was the Dutchman's, and ye was balancin' on the plank at this minit."

"Come and see for yourself," answered Wild Bill, "and give me a lift. Once in your cabin, and in front of your fire, I'll answer all the questions you may ask. But I'll answer no more until I'm inside the door."

"Ye be sartinly sober to-night," answered the Trapper, laughing, as he started down the hill, "fur ye talk sense, and that's more'n a man can do when he talks through the nozzle of a bottle.

"Lord-a-massy!" exclaimed the old man as he stood over the sled, and saw the huge box that was on it. "Lord-a-massy, Bill! what a tug ye must have had! and how ye come to be sober with sech a load behind ye is beyond the reckinin' of a man who has knowed ye nigh on to twenty year. I never knowed ye disapp'int one arter this fashion afore."

"It is strange, I confess," answered Wild Bill, appreciating the humor that lurked in the honesty of the old man's utterance. "It is strange, that's a fact, for it's Christmas Eve, and I ought to be roaring drunk at the Dutchman's this very minit, according to custom; but I pledged him to get the box through jest as he wanted it done, and that I wouldn't touch a drop of liquor until I had done it. And here it is, according to promise, for here I am sober, and here is the box."

"H'ist along, Bill, h'ist along!" exclaimed the Trapper, who suddenly became alive with interest, for he surmised whence the box had come. "H'ist along, Bill, I say, and have done with yer talkin', and let's see what ye have got on yer sled. It's strange that a man of yer sense will stand jibberin' here in the snow with a roarin' fire within a dozen rods of ye."

Whatever retort Wild Bill may have contemplated, it was effectually prevented by the energy with which the Trapper pushed the sled after him. Indeed, it was all he could do to

keep it off his heels, so earnestly did the old man propel it from
behind; and so, with many a slip and scramble on the part of
Wild Bill, and a continued muttering on the part of the Trapper about the "nonsense of a man's jibberin' in the snow arter
a twenty mile drag, with a good fire within a dozen rods of
him," the sled was shot through the doorway into the cabin,
and stood fully revealed in the bright blaze of the firelight.

"Take off yer coat and yer moccasins, Wild Bill," exclaimed
the Trapper, as he closed the door, "and git in front of the
fire; pull out the coals, and set the tea pot a-steepin'. The yarb
will take the chill out of ye better than the pizen of the Dutchman. Ye'll find a haunch of venison in the cupboard that I
roasted to-day, and some johnnycake; I doubt ef either be
cold. Help yerself, help yerself, Bill, while I take a peep at the
box."

No one can appreciate the intensity of the old man's feelings
in reference to the mysterious box, unless he calls to mind
the strictness with which he was wont to interpret and fulfill
the duties of hospitality. To him the coming of a guest was a
welcome event, and the service which the latter might require
of the host both a sacred and a pleasant obligation. To serve
a guest with his own hand, which he did with a natural courtesy peculiar to himself, was his delight. Nor did it matter
with him what the quality of the guest might be. The wandering trapper or the vagabond Indian was served with as sincere
attention as the richest visitor from the city. But now his
feelings were so stirred by the sight of the box thus strangely

brought to him, and by his surmise touching who the sender might be, that Wild Bill was left to help himself without the old man's attendance.

It was evident that Bill was equal to the occasion, and was not aware of the slightest neglect. At least, his actions were not, by the neglect of the Trapper, rendered less decided, or the quality of his appetite affected, for the examination he made of the old man's cupboard, and the familiarity with which he handled the contents, made it evident that he was not in the least abashed, or uncertain how to proceed; for he attacked the provisions with the energy of a man who had fasted long, and who has at last not only come suddenly to an ample supply of food, but also feels that for a few moments, at least, he will be unobserved. The Trapper turned toward the box, and approached it for a deliberate examination.

"The boards be sawed," he said, "and they come from the mills of the settlement, for the smoothin'-plane has been over 'em." Then he inspected the jointing, and noted how truly the edges were drawn.

"The box has come a goodly distance," he said to himself, "fur there isn't a workman this side of the Horicon that could j'int it in that fashion. There sartinly ought to be some letterin', or a leetle bit of writin', somewhere about the chest, tellin' who the box belonged to, and to whom it was sent." Saying this, the old man unlashed the box from the sled, and rolled it over, so that the side might come uppermost. As no direction appeared on the smoothly planed surface, he rolled it half over again. A little white card neatly tacked to the board was now revealed. The Trapper stooped, and on the card read, —

JOHN NORTON,

TO THE CARE OF WILD BILL.

"Yis, the 'J' be his'n," muttered the old man, as he spelled out the word J-o-h-n, "and the big 'N' be as plain as an otter-trail in the snow. The boy don't make his letters over plain, as I conceit, but the 'J' and the 'N' be his'n." And then he paused for a full minute, his head bowed over the box. "The boy don't forgit," he murmured, and he wiped his eyes with the back of his hand. "The boy don't forgit." And then he added, "No, he isn't one of the forgittin' kind. Wild Bill," said the Trapper, as he turned toward that personage, whose attack on the venison haunch was as determined as ever, "Wild Bill, this box be from Henry!"

"I shouldn't wonder," answered that individual, speaking from a mass of edibles that filled his mouth.

"And it be a Christmas gift!" continued the old man.

"It looks so," returned Bill, as laconically as before.

"And it be a mighty heavy box!" said the Trapper.

"You'd 'a' thought so, if you had dragged it over the mile-and-a-half carry. It was good sleddin' on the river, but the carry took the stuff out of me."

"Very like, very like," responded the Trapper; "fur the gullies be deep on the carry, and it must have been slippery haulin'.

Didn't ye git a leetle 'arnest in yer feelin's, Bill, afore ye got to the top of the last ridge?"

"Old man," answered Bill, as he wheeled his chair toward the Trapper, with a pint cup of tea in the one hand, and wiping his mustache with the coat sleeve of the other, " I got it to the top three times, or within a dozen feet from the top, and each time it got away from me and went to the bottom agin; for the roots was slippery, and I couldn't git a grip on the toe of my moccasins; but I held on to the rope, and I got to the bottom neck and neck with the sled every time."

"Ye did well, ye did well," responded the Trapper, laughing; "for a loaded sled goes down hill mighty fast when the slide is a steep un, and a man who gits to the bottom as quick as the sled must have a good grip, and be considerably in 'arnest. But ye got her up finally by the same path, didn't ye?"

"Yes, I got her up," returned Bill. "The fourth time I went for that ridge, I fetched her to the top, for I was madder than a hornet."

"And what did ye do, Bill?" continued the Trapper. "What did ye do when ye got to the top?"

"I jest tied that sled to a sapling so it wouldn't git away agin, and I got on to the top of that box, and I talked to that gulch a minit or two in a way that satisfied my feelings."

"I shouldn't wonder," answered the Trapper, laughing, "fur ye must have ben a good deal riled. But ye did well to git the box through, and ye got here in time, and ye've 'arnt yer wages; and now, ef ye'll tell me how much I am to pay ye, ye shall have yer money, and ye needn't scrimp yerself on the price, Wild Bill, for the drag has been a hard un; so tell me yer price, and I'll count ye out the money."

"Old man," answered Bill, "I didn't bring that box through for money, and I won't take a — "

Perhaps Wild Bill was about to emphasize his refusal by some verbal addition to the simple statement, but, if it was his intention, he checked himself, and said, "a cent."

"It's well said," answered the Trapper; "yis, it's well said, and does jestice to yer feelin's, I don't doubt; but an extra pair of breeches one of these days wouldn't hurt ye, and the money won't come amiss."

"I tell ye, old man," returned Wild Bill earnestly, "I won't take a cent. I'll allow there's several colors in my trousers, for I've patched in a dozen different pieces off and on, and I doubt, as ye hint, if the patching holds together much longer; but I've eaten at your table and slept in your cabin more than once, John Norton, and whether I've come to it sober or drunk, your door was never shut in my face; and I don't forget either that the man who sent you that box fished me from the creek one day, when I had walked into it with two bottles of the Dutchman's whisky in my pocket, and not one cent of your money or his will I take for bringing the box in to you."

"Have it yer own way, ef ye will," said the Trapper; "but I won't forgit the deed ye have did, and the boy won't forgit it neither. Come, let's clear away the vict'als, and we'll open the box. It's sartinly a big un, and I would like to see what he has put inside of it."

The opening of the box was a spectacle such as gladdens the heart to see. At such moments the countenance of the Trapper was as facile in the changefulness of its expression as that of a child. The passing feelings of his soul found an adequate mirror in his face, as the white clouds of a summer day find full reflection in the depth of a tranquil lake. He was not too old or too learned to be wise, for the wisdom of hearty happiness was his,—the wisdom of being glad, and gladly showing it.

As for Wild Bill, the best of his nature was in the ascendant, and with the curiosity and pleasure of a child, and a happiness as sincere as if the box were his own, he assisted at the opening.

"The man who made this box did the work in a workmanlike fashion," said the Trapper, as he strove to insert the edge of his hatchet into the jointing of the cover, "fur he shet these boards together like the teeth of a bear trap when the bars be well 'iled. It's a pity the boy didn't send him along with the box, Wild Bill, fur it sartinly looks as ef we should have to kindle a fire on it, and burn a hole in through the kiver."

At last, by dint of great exertion, and with the assistance of Wild Bill and the poker, the cover of the box was wrenched off, and the contents were partially revealed.

"Glory to God, Wild Bill!" exclaimed the Trapper. "Here

be yer breeches!" and he held up a pair of pantaloons made of the stoutest Scotch stuff. "Yis, here be yer breeches, fur here on the waistband be pinned a bit of paper, and on it be written, 'Fur Wild Bill.' And here be a vest to match; and here be a jacket; and here be two pairs of socks in the pocket of the jacket; and here be two woolen shirts, one packed away in each sleeve. And here!" shouted the old man, as he turned up the lapel of the coat, "Wild Bill, look here! Here be a five-dollar note!" and the old man swung one of the socks over his head, and shouted, "Hurrah for Wild Bill!" And the two hounds, catching the enthusiasm of their master, lifted their muzzles into the air, and bayed deep and long, till the cabin fairly shook with the joyful uproar of man and dogs.

It is doubtful if any gift ever took the recipient more by surprise than this bestowed upon Wild Bill. It is true that, judged by the law of strict deserts, the poor fellow had not deserved much of the world, and certainly the world had not forgotten to be strictly just in his case, for it had not given him much. It is a question if he had ever received a gift before in all his life, certainly not one of any considerable value. His reception of this generous and thoughtful provision for his wants was characteristic both of his training and his nature.

The Old Trapper, as he ended his cheering, flung the pantaloons, the vest, the jacket, the socks, the shirts, and the money into his lap.

For a moment the poor fellow sat looking at the warm and costly garments that he held in his hands, silent in an astonishment too profound for speech, and then, recovering the use of his organs, he gasped forth :—

"I swear !" and then broke down, and sobbed like a child.

The Trapper, kneeling beside the box, looked at the poor fellow with a face radiant with happiness, while his mouth was stretched with laughter, utterly unconscious that tears were brimming his own eyes.

"Old Trapper," said Wild Bill, rising to his feet, and holding the garments forth in his hands, "this is the first present I ever received in my life. I have been kicked and cussed, sneered at and taunted, and I deserved it all. But no man ever gave me a lift, or showed he cared a cent whether I starved or froze, lived or died. You know, John Norton, what a fool I've been, and what has ruined me, and that when sober I'm more of a man than many who hoot me. And here I swear, old man, that while a button is on this jacket, or two threads of these breeches hold together, I'll never touch a drop of liquor, sick or well, living or dying, so help me God ! and there's my hand on it."

"Amen !" exclaimed the Trapper, as he sprang to his feet, and clasped in his own strong palm the hand that the other had stretched out to him. "The Lord in His marcy be nigh ye when tempted, Bill, and keep ye true to yer pledge !"

Of all the pleasant sights that the angels of God, looking from their high homes, saw on earth that Christmas Eve, perhaps not one was dearer in their eyes than the spectacle here described, — the two sturdy men standing with their hands clasped in solemn pledge of the reformation of the one, and the helping sympathy of the other, above that Christmas box in the cabin in the woods.

It is not necessary to follow in detail the Trapper's further examination of the box. The reader's imagination, assisted by many a happy reminiscence, will enable him to realize the scene. There was a small keg of powder, a large plug of lead, a little chest of tea, a bag of sugar, and also one of coffee. There were nails, matches, thread, buttons, a woolen under-jacket, a pair of mittens, and a cap of choicest fur, made of an otter's skin that Henry himself had trapped a year be-fore. All these and other packages were taken out one by one, carefully examined, and characteristically commented on by the Trapper, and passed to Wild Bill, who in turn inspected and commented on them, and then laid them carefully on the table. Beneath these packages was a thin board, constituting a sort of division between its upper and lower half.

"There seems to be a sort of cellar to this box," said the Trapper, as he sat looking at the division. "I shouldn't be sur-prised ef the boy himself was in here somewhere, so be ready, Bill, fur anything, fur the Lord only knows what's underneath this board." Saying which, the old man thrust his hand under one end of the division, and pulled out a bundle loosely tied with a string, which became unfastened as the Trapper lifted the roll from its place in the box, and, as he shook it open, and held its contents at arm's length up to the light, the startled eyes of Wild Bill, and the earnest gaze of the Trapper, beheld a woman's dress!

"Heavens and 'arth, Bill!" exclaimed the Trapper, "what's this?" And then a flash of light crossed his face, in the illumination of which the look of wonder vanished, and, dropping upon his knees, he flung the dividing board out of the box, and his companion and himself saw at a glance what was underneath.

Children's shoes, and dresses of warmest stuffs; tippets and mittens; a full suit for a little boy, boots and all; a jackknife and whistle; two dolls dressed in brave finery, with flaxen hair and blue eyes; a little hatchet; a huge ball of yarn, and a hundred and one things needed in the household; and underneath all a Bible; and under that a silver star on a blue field, and pinned to the silk a scrap of paper, on which was written,—

"Hang this over the picture of the lad."

"Ay, ay," said the Trapper in a tremulous voice, as he looked at the silver star, "it shall be done as ye say, boy; but the lad has got beyond the clouds, and is walkin' a trail that is lighted from eend to eend by a light clearer and brighter than ever come from the shinin' of any star. I hope we may be found worthy to walk it with him, boy, when we, too, have come to the edge of the Great Clearin'."

To the Trapper it was perfectly evident for whom the contents of the box were intended; but the sender had left nothing in doubt, for, when the old man had lifted from the floor the board that he had flung out, he discovered some writing traced with heavy penciling on the wood, and which without much effort he spelled out to Wild Bill,—

"Give these on Christmas Day to the woman at the dismal hut, and a merry Christmas to you all."

"Ay, ay," said the Trapper, "it shall be did, barrin' accident, as ye say; and a merry Christmas it'll make fur us all. Lord-a-massy! what *will* the poor woman say when she and her leetle uns git these warm garments on? There be no trouble about fillin' the basket now; no, I sartinly can't git half of the stuff in. Wild Bill, I guess ye'll have to do some more sleddin' to-morrow, fur these presents must go over the mountain in the mornin', ef we have to harness up the pups." And then he told his companion of the poor woman and the children, and his intended visit to them on the morrow.

"I fear," he said, "that they be havin' a hard time of it, 'specially ef her husband has desarted her."

"Little good he would do her, if he was with her," answered Wild Bill, "for he's a lazy knave when he is sober, and a thief as well, as you and I know, John Norton; for he's fingered our traps more than once, and swapped the skins for liquor at the Dutchman's; but he's thieved once too many times, for the folks in the settlement has ketched him in the act, and they put him in the jail for six months, as I heard day before yesterday."

"I'm glad on't; yis, I'm glad on't," answered the Trapper; "and I hope they'll keep him there till they've larnt him how to work. I've had my eye on the knave for a good while, and the last time I seed him I told him ef he fingered any more of my traps, I'd larn him the commandments in a way he wouldn't

"On the other side of the mountain stood the dismal hut."

forgit; and, as I had him in hand, and felt a leetle like talkin'
that mornin', I gin him a piece of my mind, techin' his treatment of his wife and leetle uns, that he didn't relish, I fancy,
fur he winced and squirmed like a fox in a trap. Yis, I'm glad
they've got the knave, and I hope they'll keep him till he's answered fur his misdoin'; but I'm sartinly afeered the poor woman be havin' a hard time of it."

"I fear so, too," answered Wild Bill; "and if I can do anything to help you in your plans, jest say the word, and I'm
your man to back or haul, jest as you want me."

And so it was arranged that they should go over the mountain together on the morrow, and take the provisions and the
gifts that were in the box to the poor woman. And, after talking
awhile of the happiness their visit would give, the two men,
happy in their thoughts, and with their hearts full of that peace
which passeth the understanding of the selfish, laid themselves
down to sleep; and over the two, — the one drawing to the
close of an honorable and well-spent life, the other standing at
the middle of a hitherto useless existence, but facing the future
with a noble resolution, — over the two, as they slept, the angels
of Christmas kept their watch.

II.

On the other side of the mountain stood the dismal hut; and
the stars of that blessed eve had shone down upon the lonely
clearing in which it stood, and the smooth white surface of the

frozen and snow-covered lake which lay in front of it, as brightly as they had shone on the cabin of the Trapper; but no friendly step had made its trail in the surrounding snow, and no blessed gift had been brought to its solitary door.

As the evening wore on, the great clearing round about it remained drearily void of sound or motion, and filled only with the white stillness of the frosty, snow-lighted night. Once, indeed, a wolf stole from underneath the dark balsams into the white silence, and, running up a huge log that lay aslant a ledge of rocks, looked across and round the great opening in the woods, stood a moment, then gave a shivering sort of a yelp, and scuttled back under the shadow of the forest, as if its darkness was warmer than the frozen stillness of the open space. An owl, perched somewhere amid the pine-tops, snug and warm within the cover of its arctic plumage, engaged from time to time in solemn gossip with some neighbor that lived on the opposite shore of the lake. And once a raven, roosting on the dry bough of a lightning-blasted pine, dreamed that the white moonlight was the light of dawn, and began to stir his sable wings, and croak a harsh welcome; but awakened by his blunder, and ashamed of his mistake, he broke off in the very midst of his discordant call, and again settled gloomily down amid his black plumes to his interrupted repose, making by his sudden silence the surrounding silence more silent than before.

It seemed as if the very angels, who, we are taught, fly abroad over all the earth that blessed night, carrying gifts to every household, had forgotten the cabin in the woods, and had left it to the cold hospitality of unsympathetic nature.

Within the lonely hut, which thus seemed forgotten of Heaven itself, sat a woman huddling her young — two girls and a boy. The fireplace was of monstrous proportions, and the chimney yawned upward so widely that one looking up the sooty passage might see the stars shining overhead. A little fire burned feebly in the huge stone recess : scant warmth might such a fire yield, kindled in such a fireplace, to those around it. Indeed, the little flame seemed conscious of its own inability, and burned with a wavering and mistrustful flicker, as if it were discouraged in view of the task set before it, and had more than half concluded to go out altogether.

The cabin was of large size, and undivided into apartments. The little fire was only able to illuminate the central section, and more than half of the room was hidden in utter darkness. The woman's face, which the faint flame over which she was crouched revealed with painful clearness, showed pale and haggard. The induration of exposure and the tightening lines of hunger sharpened and marred a countenance which a happier fortune would have kept even comely. It had that old look about it which comes from wretchedness rather than age, and the weariness of its expression was pitiful to see. Was it work or vain waiting for happier fortunes that made her look so tired ? Alas ! the weariness of waiting for what we long for, and long for purely, but which never comes ! Is it the work or the longing — the long longing — that has put the silver in your

3

head, friend, and scarred the smooth bloom of your cheeks, my lady, with those ugly lines?

"Mother, I'm hungry," said the little boy, looking up into the woman's face. "Can't I have just a little more to eat?"

"Be still," answered the woman sharply, speaking in the tones of vexed inability. "I've given you almost the last morsel in the house."

The boy said nothing more, but nestled up more closely to his mother's knee, and stuck one little stockingless foot out until the cold toes were half hidden in the ashes. O warmth! blessed warmth! how pleasant art thou to old and young alike! Thou art the emblem of life, as thy absence is the evidence and sign of life's cold opposite. Would that all the cold toes in the world could get to my grate to-night, and all the shivering ones be gathered to this fireside! Ay, and that the children of poverty, that lack for bread, might get their hungry hands into that well-filled cupboard there, too!

In a moment the woman said, "You children had better go to bed. You'll be warmer in the rags than in this miserable fireplace."

The words were harshly spoken, as if the very presence of the children, cold and hungry as they were, was a vexation to her; and they moved off in obedience to her command.

O cursed poverty! I know thee to be of Satan, for I myself have eaten at thy scant table, and slept in thy cold bed. And never yet have I seen thee bring one smile to human lips, or dry one tear as it fell from a human eye. But I have seen thee sharpen the tongue for biting speech, and harden the tender heart. Ay, I've seen thee make even the presence of love a burden, and cause the mother to wish that the puny babe nursing her scant breast had never been born. And so the children went to their unsightly bed, and silence reigned in the hut.

"Mother," said one of the girls, speaking out of the darkness,— "mother, isn't this Christmas Eve?"

"Yes," answered the woman sharply. "Go to sleep." And again there was silence.

Happy is childhood, that amid whatever deprivation and misery it can so weary itself in the day that when night comes on it can lose in the forgetfulness of slumber its sorrows and wants!

Thus, while the children lost the sense of their unhappy surroundings, including the keen pangs of hunger, for a time, and under the tattered blankets that covered them saw, perhaps, visions of enchanting lands, and in their dreams feasted at those wonderful tables which hungry children see only in sleep, to the poor woman sitting at the failing fire there came no surcease of sorrow, and no vision threw even an evanescent brightness over the hard, cold facts of her surroundings. And the reality of her condition was dire enough, God knows. Alone in the wilderness, miles from any human habitation, the trails covered deep with snow, her provisions exhausted, actual suffering already upon them, and starvation staring them squarely in the face,— no wonder that her soul sank within her; no wonder that her thoughts turned toward bitterness.

"Yes, it's Christmas Eve," she muttered, "and the rich will keep it gayly. God sends them presents enough; but you see if He remembers me! Oh, they may talk about the angels of Christmas Eve flying abroad to-night, loaded with gifts, but they'll fly mighty high above this shanty, I reckon; no, they won't even drop a piece of meat as they soar past." And so she sat muttering and moaning over her woes, and they were heavy enough,— too heavy for her poor soul, unassisted, to lift, — while the flame on the hearth grew thinner and thinner, until it had no more warmth in it than the shadow of a ghost, and, like its resemblance, was about to flit and fade away. At last she said, in a softened tone, as if the remembrance of the Christmas legend had softened her surly thoughts and sweetened the bitter mood:—

"Perhaps I'm wrong to take on so. Perhaps it isn't God's fault that I and my children are deserted and starving. But why should the innocent be punished for the guilty, and why should the wicked have enough and to spare, while those who do no evil go half naked and starved?"

Alas, poor woman! that puzzle has puzzled many besides thee, and many lips besides thine have asked that question, querulously or entreatingly, many a time; but whether they asked it in vexation and rebellion of spirit, or humbly besought Heaven to answer, to neither murmur nor prayer did Heaven vouchsafe a response. Is it because we are so small, or, being small, are so inquisitive, that the Great Oracle of the blue remains so dumb when we cry?

At this point the poor little flame, as if unable to abide the cold much longer, flared fitfully, and uneasily shifted itself from brand to brand, threatening with many a flicker to go out; but the woman, with her elbows on her knees, and her face settled firmly between her hands, still sat with eyes that saw not the feeble flame at which they so steadily gazed.

"I will do it, *I will do it!*" she suddenly exclaimed. "I will make one more effort. They shall not starve while I have strength to try. Perhaps God will aid me. They say He always does at the last pinch, and He certainly sees that I am there now. I wonder if He's been waiting for me to get just where I am before He helped me. There is one more chance left, and I'll make the trial. I'll go down to the shore where I saw the big tracks in the snow. It's a long way, but I shall get there somehow. If God is going to be good to me, He won't let me freeze or faint on the way. Yes, I'll creep into bed now, and try to get a little sleep, for I must be strong in the morning." And with these words the poor woman crept off to her bed, and burrowed down, more like an animal than a human being, beside her little ones, as they lay huddled close together and asleep, down in the rags.

What angel was it that followed her to her miserable couch, and stirred kindly feelings in her bosom? Some sweet one, surely; for she shortly lifted herself to a sitting posture, and, gently drawing down the old blanket with which the children, for warmth's sake, had wrapped their heads, looked as only a mother might at the three little faces lying side by side, and, bending tenderly over them, she placed a gentle kiss upon the forehead of each; then she nestled down again in her own place, and said, "Perhaps God will help me." And with this sentence, half a prayer and half a doubt, born on the one hand from that sweet faith which never quite deserts a woman's bosom, and on the other from that bitter experience which had made her seem in her own eyes deserted of God, she fell asleep.

She, too, dreamed; but her dreaming was only the prolongation of her waking thoughts; for long after her eyes closed she moved uneasily on her hard couch, and muttered, "Perhaps God will. Perhaps —"

Sad is it for us who are old enough to have tasted the bitterness of that cup which life sooner or later presents to all lips, and have borne the burden of its toil and fretting, that our vexations and disappointments pursue us even in our slumber, disturbing our sleep with reproachful visions and the sound of voices whose upbraiding robs us of our otherwise peaceful repose. Perhaps somewhere in the years to come, after much wandering and weariness, guided of God, we may come to that fountain of which the ancients dreamed, and for which the noblest among them sought so long, and died seeking; plunging into which, we shall find our lost youth in its cool depths, and, rising refreshed and strengthened, shall go on our eternal journey re-clothed with the beauty, the innocence, and the happiness of our youth.

The poor woman slept uneasily, and with much muttering to

herself; but the rapid hours slid noiselessly down the icy grooves of night, and soon the cold morning put its white face against the frozen windows of the east, and peered shiveringly forth. Who says the earth cannot look as cold and forbidding as the human countenance? The sky hung over the frozen world like a dome of gray steel, whose invisibly matched plates were riveted here and there by a few white, gleaming stars. The surface of the snow sparkled with crystals that flashed colorlessly cold. The air seemed armed, and full of sharp, eager points that pricked the skin painfully. The great tree-trunks cracked their sharp protests against the frosty entrances being made beneath their bark. The lake, from under the smothering ice, roared in dismay and pain, and sent the thunders of its wrath at its imprisonment around the resounding shores. A bitter morn, a bitter morn, — ah me! a bitter morn for the poor!

The woman, wakened by the gray light, moved in the depths of the tattered blankets, sat upright, rubbed her eyes with her hands, looked about her as if to recall her scattered senses, and then, as thought returned, crept stealthily out of the hole in which she had lain, that she might not wake the children, who, coiled together, slumbered on, still closely clasped in the arms of blessed unconsciousness.

"They had better sleep," she said to herself. "If I fail to bring them meat, I hope they will never wake!"

Ah! if the poor woman could only have foreseen the bitter disappointment, or that other something which the future was to bring her, would she have made that prayer? Is it best for us, as some say, that we cannot see what is coming, but must weep on till the last tear is shed, uncheered by the sweet fortune so nigh, or laugh unchecked until the happy tones are mingled with, and smothered by, the rising moan? Is it best, I wonder?

She noiselessly gathered together what additions she could make to her garments, and then, taking down the rifle from its hangings, opened the door, and stepped forth into the outer cold. There was a look of brave determination in her eyes as she faced the chilly greeting the world gave her, and, with more of hopefulness than had before appeared upon her countenance, she struck bravely off along the lake shore, which at this point receded toward the mountain.

For an hour she kept steadily on, with her eyes constantly on the alert for the least sign of the wished and prayed-for game. Suddenly she stopped, and crouched down in the snow, peering straight ahead. Well might she seek concealment, for there, standing on a point of land that jutted sharply out into the lake, not forty rods away, unscreened and plain to view, stood a buck of such goodly proportions as one even in years of hunting might not see.

The woman's eyes fairly gleamed as she saw the noble animal standing thus in full sight; but who may tell the agony of fear and hope that filled her bosom! The buck stood lordly erect, facing the east, as if he would do homage to, or receive homage from, the rising sun, whose yellow beams fell full upon

his uplifted front. The thought of her mind, the fear of her
heart, were plain. The buck would soon move; when he moved,
which way would he move? Would he go from or come toward
her? Would she get him, or would she lose him? Oh, the agony
of that thought!

"God of the starving," burst from her quivering lips, "let
not my children die!"

Many prayers more ornate rose that day to Him whose ears
are open to all cries. But of all that prayed on that Christmas
morn, whether with few words or many, surely, no heart rose
with the seeking words more earnestly than that of the poor
woman kneeling as she prayed, rifle in hand, amid the snow.

"God of the starving, let not my children die!"

That was her prayer; and, as if in answer to her agonizing
petition, the buck turned and began to advance directly toward
her, browsing as he came. Once he stopped, looked around, and
snuffed the air suspiciously. Had he scented her presence, and
would he bound away? Should she fire now? No; her judg-
ment told her she could not trust the gun or her aim at such a
range. He must come nigher,— come even to the big maple,
and stand there, not ten rods away; then she felt sure she
should get him. So she waited. Oh, how the cold ate into
her! How her teeth chattered as the chills ran their torturing
courses through her thin, shivering frame! But still she clutched
the cold barrel, and still she watched and waited, and still she
prayed :—

"God of the starving, let not my children die!"

Alas, poor woman! My own body shivers as I think of thine, and my pen falters to write what misery befell thee on that wretchd morn.

Did the buck turn? Did he, having come so tantalizingly near, retrace his steps? No. He continued to advance. Had Heaven heard her prayer? Her soul answered it had; and with such feelings in it toward Him to whom she had appealed as she had not felt in all her life before, she steadied herself for the shot. For even as she prayed, the deer came on, — came to the big maple, and lifted his muzzle to its highest reach to seize with his tongue a thin streamer of moss that lay against the smooth bark. There he stood, his blue-brown side full toward her, unconscious of her presence. Noiselessly she cocked the piece. Noiselessly she raised it to her face, and, with every nerve drawn to its tightest tension, sighted the noble game, and — *fired*.

Had the frosty air watered her eye? was it a tear of joy and gratitude that dimmed the clearness of its sight? or were the half-frozen fingers unable to steady the cold barrel at the instant of its explosion? We know not. We only know that in spite of prayer, in spite of noblest effort, she missed the game. For, as the rifle cracked, the buck gave a snort of fear, and with swift bounds flew up the mountain; while the poor woman, dropping the gun with a groan, fell fainting on the snow.

III.

At the same moment the rifle sounded, two men, the Trapper with his pack, and Wild Bill with his sled heavily loaded, were descending the western slope of the mountain, not a mile from the clearing in which stood the lonely cabin. The sound of the piece brought them to a halt as quickly as if the bullet had cut through the air in front of their faces. For several minutes both stood in the attitude of listening.

"Down into the snow with ye, pups!" exclaimed the Trapper, in a hoarse whisper. "Down into the snow with ye, I say! Rover, ef ye lift yer muzzle agin, I'll warm yer back with the ramrod. By the Lord, Bill, the buck is comin' this way; ye can see his horns lift above the leetle balsams as he breaks through the thicket yender. Ef he strikes the runway, he'll sartinly come within range;" and the Old Trapper slipped his arms from the pack, and, lowering it to the earth, sank on his knees beside it, where he waited as motionless as if the breath had departed his body.

Onward came the game. As the Trapper had suggested, the buck, with mighty and far-reaching bounds, cleared the shrubby obstructions, and, entering the runway, tore up the familiar path with the violence of a tornado. Onward he came, his head flung upward, his antlers laid well back, tongue lolling from his mouth, and his nostrils smoking with the hot breaths that burst in streaming columns from them. Not until his swift career had brought him exactly in front of his position did the old man stir a muscle. But then, quick as the motion of the leaping game, his rifle jumped to his cheek, and even as the buck was at the central point of his leap, and suspended in the air, the piece cracked sharp and clear, and the deer, stricken to his death, fell with a crash to the ground. The quivering hounds rose to their feet, and bayed long and deep; Wild Bill swung his hat and yelled; and for a moment the woods rang with the wild cries of dogs and man.

"Lord-a-massy, Bill, what a mouth ye have when ye open it!" exclaimed the Trapper, as he leisurely poured the powder into the still smoking barrel. "Atween ye and the pups, it's enough to drive a man crazy. I should sartinly think ye had never seed a deer shot afore, by the way ye be actin'."

"I've seen a good many, as you know, John Norton; but I never saw one tumbled over by a single bullet when at the very top of his jump, as that one was. I surely thought you had waited too long, and I wouldn't have given a cent for your chances when you pulled. It was a wonderful shot, John Norton, and I would take just such another tramp as I have had, to see you do it again, old man."

"It wasn't bad," returned the Trapper; "no, it sartinly wasn't bad, for he was goin' as ef the Old Harry was arter him. I shouldn't wonder ef he had felt the tech of lead down there in the holler, and the smart of his hurt kept him flyin'. Let's go and look him over, and see ef we can't find the markin's of the bullit on him."

In a moment the two stood above the dead deer.

"It is as I thought," said the Trapper, as he pointed with his ramrod to a stain of blood on one of the hams of the buck. "The bullit drove through his thigh here, but it didn't tech the bone, and was a sheer waste of lead, fur it only sot him goin' like an arrer. Bill, I sartinly doubt," continued the old man, as he measured the noble animal with his eye, "I sartinly doubt ef I ever seed a bigger deer. There's seven prongs on his horns, and I'd bet a horn of powder agin a chargerful that he'd weigh three hunderd pounds as he lies. Lord! what a Christmas gift he'll be fur the woman! The skin will make a blanket fit fur a queen to sleep under, and the meat, jediciously cared fur, will last her all winter. We must manage to git it to the edge of the clearin', anyhow, or the wolves might make free with our venison, Bill. Yer sled is a strong un, and it'll bear the loadin', ef ye go keerful."

The Trapper and his companion set themselves to their task with the energy of men accustomed to surmount every obstacle, and in a short half-hour the sled, with its double loading, stopped at the door of the lonely cabin.

"I don't understand this, Wild Bill," said the Trapper. "Here be a woman's tracks in the snow, and the door be left a leetle ajar, but there be no smoke in the chimney, and they sartinly ain't very noisy inside. I'll jest give a knock or two, and see ef they be stirrin';" and, suiting the action to the word, he knocked long and loud on the large door. But to his noisy summons there came no response, and without a moment of farther hesitation he shoved open the door, and entered.

"God of marcy! Wild Bill," exclaimed the Trapper, "look in here."

A huge room dimly lighted, holes in the roof, here and there a heap of snow on the floor, an immense fireplace with no fire in it, and a group of scared, wild-looking children huddled together in the farther corner, like young and timid animals that had fled in affright from the nest where they had slept, at some fearful intrusion. That is what the Trapper saw.

"I"— Whatever Wild Bill was about to say, his astonishment, and, we may add, his pity, were too profound for him to complete his ejaculation.

"Don't ye be afeerd, leetle uns," said the Trapper, as he advanced into the center of the room to survey more fully the wretched place. "This be Christmas morn, and me and Wild Bill and the pups have come over the mountain to wish ye all a merry Christmas. But where be yer mother?" queried the old man, as he looked kindly at the startled group.

"We don't know where she is," answered the older of the two girls; "we thought she was in bed with us, till you woke us. We don't know where she has gone."

"I have it, I have it, Wild Bill!" exclaimed the Trapper, whose eyes had been busy scanning the place while talking with the children. "The rifle be gone from the hangin's, and the tracks in the snow be hern. Yis, yis, I see it all. She went out in hope of gittin' the leetle uns here somethin' to eat, and that was her rifle we heerd, and her bullit made that hole in the ham of the buck. What a disapp'intment to the poor creetur when she seed she hadn't hit him! Her heart eena'-most broke, I dare say. But the Lord was in it — leastwise, He didn't go agin the proper shapin' of things arterwards. Come, Bill, let's stir round lively, and git the shanty in shape a leetle, and some vict'als on the table afore she comes. Yis, git out your axe, and slash into that dead beech at the corner of the cabin, while I sorter clean up inside. A fire is the fust thing on sech a mornin' as this; so scurry round, Bill, and bring in the wood as ef ye was a good deal in 'arnest, and do ye cut to the measure of the fireplace, and don't waste yer time in shorten-in' it, fur the longer the fireplace, the longer the wood; that is, ef ye want to make it a heater."

His companion obeyed with alacrity; and by the time the Trapper had cleaned out the snow, and swept down the soot from the sides of the fireplace, and put things partially to rights, Bill had stacked the dry logs into the huge opening, nearly to the upper jamb, and, with the help of some large sheets of birch bark, kindled them to a flame. "Come here, leetle uns," said the Trapper, as he turned his good-natured face toward the children,— "come here, and put yer leetle feet on the h'arth-stun, fur it's warmin', and I conceit yer toes be about freezin'."

It was not in the power of children to withstand the attrac-tion of such an invitation, extended with such a hearty voice and such benevolence of feature. The children came promptly forward, and stood in a row on the great stone, and warmed their little shivering bodies by the abundant flames.

"Now, leetle folks," said the Trapper, "jest git yerselves

well warmed, then git on what clothes ye've got, and we'll have some breakfast,—yis, we'll have breakfast ready by the time yer mother gits back, fur I know where she be gone, and she'll be hungry and cold when she gits in. I don't conceit that this leetle chap here can help much, but ye girls be big enough to help a good deal. So, when ye be warm, do ye put away the bed to the furderest corner, and shove out the table in front of the fire, and put on the dishes, sech as ye have, and be smart about it, too, fur yer mother will sartinly be comin' soon, and we must be ahead of her with the cookin'."

What a change the next half-hour made in the appearance of the cabin! The huge fire sent its heat to the farthest corner of the great room. The miserable bed had been removed out of sight, and the table, drawn up in front of the fire, was set with the needed dishes. On the hearthstone a large platter of venison steak, broiled by the Trapper's skill, simmered in the heat. A mighty pile of cakes, brown to a turn, flanked one side, while a stack of potatoes baked in the ashes supported the other. The teapot sent forth its refreshing odor through the room. The children, with their faces washed and hair partially, at least, combed, ran about with bare feet on the warm floor, comfortable and happy. To them it was as a beautiful dream. The breakfast was ready, and the visitors sat waiting for the coming of her to whose assistance the angel of Christmas Eve had sent them.

"Sh!" whispered the Trapper, whose quick ear had caught the sound of a dragging step in the snow. "She's comin'!"

Too weary and faint, too sick at heart and exhausted in body to observe the unaccustomed signs of human presence around her dwelling, the poor woman dragged herself to the door, and opened it. The gun she still held in her hand fell rattling to the floor, and, with eyes wildly opened, she gazed bewildered at the spectacle. The blazing fire, the set table, the food on the hearthstone, the smiling children, the two men! She passed her hands across her eyes as one waking from sleep. Was she dreaming? Was this cabin the miserable hut she had left at daybreak? Was that the same fireplace in front of whose cold and cheerless recess she had crouched the night before? And were those two strangers there men, or were they angels? Was what she saw real, or was it only a fevered vision born of her weakness?

Her senses actually reeled to and fro, and she trembled for a moment on the verge of unconsciousness. Indeed, the shock was so overwhelming that in another instant she would have swooned and fallen to the floor had not the growing faintness been checked by the sound of a human voice.

"A merry Christmas to ye, my good woman," said the Trapper. "A merry Christmas to ye and yourn!"

The woman started as the hearty tones fell on her ear, and, steadying herself by the door, she said, speaking as one partially dazed :—

"Are you John Norton the Trapper, or are you an ang—"

"Ye needn't sight agin," interrupted the old man. "Yis, I'm old John Norton himself, nothin' better and nothin' wuss; and

4

the man in the chair here by my side is Wild Bill, and ye couldn't make an angel out of him, ef ye tried from now till next Christmas. Yis, my good woman, I'm John Norton, and this is Wild Bill, and we've come over the mountain to wish ye a merry Christmas, ye and yer leetle uns, and help ye keep the day; and, ye see, we've been stirrin' a leetle in yer absence, and breakfast be waitin'. Wild Bill and me will jest go out and cut a leetle more wood, while ye warm and wash yerself; and when ye be ready to eat, ye may call us, and we'll see which can git into the house fust."

So saying the Trapper, followed by his companion, passed out of the door, while the poor woman, without a word, moved toward the fire, and, casting one look at her children, at the table, at the food on the hearthstone, dropped on her knees by a chair, and buried her face in her hands.

"I say," said Wild Bill to the Trapper, as he crept softly away from the door, to which he had returned to shut it more closely, "I say, John Norton, the woman is on her knees by a chair."

"Very likely, very likely," returned the old man reverently; and then he began to chop vigorously at a huge log, with his back toward his comrade.

Perhaps some of you who read this tale will come sometime, when weary and heart-sick, to something drearier than an empty house, some bleak, cold day, some lonely morn, and with a starving heart and benumbed soul,— ay, and empty-handed, too,— enter in only to find it swept and garnished, and what you most needed and longed for waiting for you. Then will you, too, drop upon your knees, and cover your face with your hands, ashamed that you had murmured against the hardness of your lot, or forgotten the goodness of Him who suffered you to be tried only that you might more fully appreciate the triumph.

"My good woman," said the Trapper, when the breakfast was eaten, "we've come, as we said, to spend the day with ye; and accordin' to custom — and a pleasant un it be fur sartin — we've brought ye some presents. A good many of them come from him who called on ye as he and me passed through the lake last fall. I dare say ye remember him, and he sartinly has remembered ye. Fur last evenin', when I was makin' up a leetle pack to bring ye myself, — fur I conceited I had better come over and spend the day with ye, — Wild Bill came to my door with a box on his sled that the boy had sent in from his home in the city; and in the box he had put a great many presents fur him and me; and in the lower half of the box he had put a good many presents fur ye and yer leetle uns, and we've brought them all over with us. Some of the things be fur eatin' and some of them be fur wearin'; and that there may be no misunderstandin', I would say that all the things that be in the pack-basket there, and all the things that be on the sled, too, belong to ye. And as I see the wood-pile isn't a very big un fur this time of the year, Bill and me be goin' out to settle our breakfast a leetle with the axes. And while we be gone, I conceit ye had better rummage the things over, and them that be good fur eatin' ye had better put in the cupboard, and them that be good fur wearin' ye had better put on yerself and yer leetle uns ; and then we'll all be ready to make a fair start. Fur this be Christmas Day, and we be goin' to keep it as it orter be kept. Ef we've had sorrers, we'll forgit 'em ; and we'll laugh, and eat, and be merry. Fur this be Christmas, my good woman ! children, this be Christmas ! Wild Bill, my boy, this be Christmas ; and, pups, this be Christmas ! And we'll all laugh, and eat, and be merry."

The joyfulness of the old man was contagious. His happiness flowed over as waters flow over the rim of a fountain. Wild Bill laughed as he seized his axe, the woman rose from the table smiling, the girls giggled, the little boy stamped, and the hounds, catching the spirit of their merry master, swung their tails round, and bayed in canine gladness ; and amid the joyful uproar the Old Trapper spun himself out of the door, and chased Wild Bill through the snow like a boy.

The dinner was to be served at two o'clock ; and what a dinner it was, and what preparations preceded ! The snow had been shoveled from around the cabin, the holes in the roof roughly but effectually thatched. A good pile of wood was stacked in front of the doorway. The spring that bubbled from the bank had been cleared of ice, and a protection constructed over it. The huge buck had been dressed, and hung high above the reach of wolves. Cedar and balsam branches had been placed in the corners and along the sides of the room. Great sprays of the tasseled pine and the feathery tamarack were suspended from the ceiling. The table had been enlarged, and extra seats extemporized. The long-unused oven had been cleaned out, and under its vast dome the red flames flashed and rolled upward. What a change a few hours had brought to that lonely cabin and its wretched inmates! The woman, dressed in her new garments, her hair smoothly combed, her face lighted with smiles, looked positively comely. The girls, happy in their fine clothes and marvelous toys, danced round the room, wild with delight; while the little boy strutted about the floor in his new boots, proudly showing them to each person for the hundredth time.

The hostess's attention was equally divided between the temperature of the oven and the adornment of the table. A snow-white sheet, one of a dozen she had found in the box, was drafted peremptorily into service, and did duty as a tablecloth. Oh, the innocent and funny makeshifts of poverty, and the goodly distance it can make a little go! Perhaps some of us, as we stand in our rich dining rooms, and gaze with pride at the silver, the gold, the cut glass, and the transparent china, can recall a little kitchen in a homely house far away, where our good mothers once set their tables for their guests, and what a brave show the few extra dishes made when they brought them out on the rare festive days.

However it might strike you, fair reader, to the poor woman and her guests there was nothing incongruous in a sheet serving as a tablecloth. Was it not white and clean and properly shaped, and would it not have been a tablecloth if it hadn't

been a sheet? How very nice and particular some people can
be over the trifling matter of a name! And this sheet had no
right to be a sheet, since any one with half an eye could see at
a glance that it was predestined from the first to be a tablecloth,
for it sat as smoothly on the wooden surface as pious looks on a
deacon's face, while the easy and nonchalant way it draped itself
at the corners was perfectly jaunty.

The edges of this square of white sheeting that had thus
providentially found its true and predestined use were orna-
mented with the leaves of the wild myrtle, stitched on in the
form of scallops. In the center, with a brave show of artistic
skill, were the words, "Merry Christmas," prettily worked with
the small brown cones of the pines. This, the joint product of
Wild Bill's industry and the woman's taste, commanded the
enthusiastic admiration of all; and even the little boy, from the
height of a chair into which he had climbed, was profoundly
affected by the show it made.

The Trapper had charge of the meat department, and it is
safe to say that no Delmonico could undertake to serve venison
in greater variety than did he. To him it was a grand occasion,
and — in a culinary sense — he rose grandly to meet it. What
bosom is without its little vanities? and shall we laugh at the
dear old man because he looked upon the opportunity before
him with feeling other than pure benevolence, — even of com-
placency that what he was doing was being done as no one
else could do it?

There was venison roasted, and venison broiled, and venison

fried ; there was hashed venison, and venison spitted ; there was a side-dish of venison sausage, strong with the odor of sage, and slightly dashed with wild thyme ; and a huge kettle of soup, on whose rich creamy surface pieces of bread and here and there a slice of potato floated.

"I tell ye, Bill," said the Trapper to his companion, as he stirred the soup with a long ladle, "this pot isn't act'ally runnin' over with taters, but ye can see a bit occasionally ef ye look sharp and keep the ladle goin' round pretty lively. No, the taters ain't over plenty," continued the old man, peering into the pot, and sinking his voice to a whisper, "but there wasn't but fifteen in the bag, and the woman took twelve of 'em fur her kittle, and ye can't make three taters look act'ally crowded in two gallons of soup, can ye, Bill ?" And the old man punched that personage in the ribs with the thumb of the hand that was free from service, while he kept the ladle going with the other.

"Lord !" exclaimed the Trapper, speaking to Bill, who, having taken a look into the old man's kettle, was digging his knuckles into his eyes to free them from the spray that was jetted into them from the fountains of mirth within that were now in full play, — "Lord ! ef there isn't another piece of tater gone all to pieces ! Bill, ef I make another circle with this ladle, there won't be a whole slice left, and ye'll swear there wasn't a tater in the soup." And the two men, with their faces within twenty inches, laughed and laughed like boys.

How sweet it is to think that when the Maker set up this

strange instrument we call ourselves, and strung it for service,
He selected of the heavy chords so few, and of the lighter ones
so many! Some muffled ones there are; some slow and solemn
sounds swell sadly forth at intervals, but blessed be God that we
are so easily tickled, and the world is so funny that within it,
even when exiled from home and friends, we find, as the days
come and go, the causes and occasions of hilarity!

Wild Bill had been placed in charge of the liquids. What a
satire there is in circumstances, and how those of to-day laugh
at those of yesterday! Yes, Wild Bill had charge of the liquids,
— no mean charge, when the occasion is considered. Nor was
the position without its embarrassments, as few honorable posi-
tions are, for it brought him face to face with the problem of
the day — dishes; for, between the two cooks of the occasion,
every dish in the cabin had been brought into requisition, and
poor Bill was left in the predicament of having to make tea
and coffee with no pots to make them in.

But Bill was not lacking in wit, if he was in pots, and he
solved the conundrum how to make tea without a teapot in a
manner that extorted the woman's laughter, and commanded
the Old Trapper's admiration.

In ransacking the lofts above the apartment, he had lighted
on several large stone jugs, which, with the courage — shall we
call it the audacity? — of genius, he had seized upon; and,
having thoroughly rinsed them, and freed them from certain
odors,— with which we are free to say Bill was more or less familiar,— he brought them forward as substitutes for kettle and

pot. Indeed, they worked admirably, for in them the berry and the leaves might not only be properly steeped, but the flavor could be retained beyond what it might in many of our famous and high-sounding patented articles.

But Bill, while ingenious and courageous to the last degree, was lacking in education, especially in scientific directions. He had never been made acquainted with that great promoter of modern civilization — the expansive properties of steam. The corks he had whittled out for his bravely extemporized tea and coffee pots were of the closest fit; and, as they had been inserted with the energy of a man who, having conquered a serious difficulty, is determined to reap the full benefit of his triumph, there was at least no danger that the flavor of the concoctions would escape through any leakage at the muzzle. Having thus prepared them for steeping, he placed the jugs in his corner of the fireplace, and pushed them well up through the ashes to the live coals.

"Wild Bill," said the Trapper, who wished to give his companion the needed warning in as delicate and easy a manner as possible, "Wild Bill, ye have sartinly got the right idee techin' the makin' of tea and coffee, fur the yarb should be steeped, and the berry, too,— leastwise, arter it's biled up once or twice, — and therefore it be only reasonable that the nozzles should be closed moderately tight; but a man wants considerable experience in the business, or he's likely to overdo it jest a leetle, and ef ye don't cut some slots in them wooden corks ye've driven into them nozzles, Bill, there'll be a good deal of tea and coffee floatin' round in yer corner of the fireplace afore many minits, and I conceit there'll be a man about yer size lookin' fur a couple of corks and pieces of jugs out there in the clearin', too."

"Do you think so?" answered Bill, incredulously. "Don't you be scared, old man, but keep on stirring your soup and turning the meat, and I'll keep my eye on the bottles."

"That's right, Bill," returned the Trapper; "ye keep yer eye right on 'em, specially on that un that's furderest in toward the butt of the beech log there; fur ef there's any vartue in signs, that jug be gittin' oneasy. Yis," continued the old man, after a minute's pause, during which his eye hadn't left the jug, "yis, that jug will want more room afore many minits, ef I'm any jedge, and I conceit I had better give it the biggest part of the fireplace;" and the Trapper hastily moved the soup and his half-dozen plates of cooked meats to the other end of the hearth-stone, whither he retired himself, like one who, feeling that he is called upon to contend with unknown forces, wisely beats a retreat. He even put himself behind a stack of wood that lay piled up in his corner, like one who does not despise, in a sudden emergency, an artificial protection.

"Bill," called the Trapper, "edge round a leetle, — edge round, and git in closer to the jamb. It's sheer foolishness standin' where ye be, fur the water will be wallopin' in a minit, and ef the corks be swelled in the nozzle, there'll be an explosion. Git in toward the jamb, and watch the ambushment under kiver."

"Old man," answered Bill, as he turned his back carelessly toward the fireplace, "I've got the bearin's of this trail, and know what I'm about. The jugs are as strong as iron kittles, and I ain't afraid of their bust—"

Bill never finished the sentence, for the explosion predicted by the Trapper occurred. It was a tremendous one, and the huge fireplace was filled with flying brands, ashes, and clouds of steam. The Trapper ducked his head, the woman screamed, and the hounds rushed howling to the farthest end of the room; while Bill, with half a somersault, disappeared under the table.

"Hurrah!" shouted the Trapper, lifting his head from behind the wood, and critically surveying the scene. "Hurrah, Bill!" he shouted, as he swung the ladle over his head. "Come out from under the table, and man yer battery agin. Yer old mortars was loaded to the muzzle, and ef ye had depressed the pieces a leetle, ye'd 'a' blowed the cabin to splinters; as it was, the chimney got the biggest part of the chargin', and ye'll find yer rammers on the other side of the mountain."

It was, in truth, a scene of uproarious hilarity; for once the explosion was over, and the woman and children saw there was no danger, and apprehended the character of the performance, they joined unrestrainedly in the Trapper's laughter, in which they were assisted by Wild Bill, as if he were not the victim of his own over-confidence.

"I say, Old Trapper," he called from under the table, "did both guns go off? I was getting under cover when the battery opened, and didn't notice whether the firing was in sections or along the whole line. If there's a piece left, I think I will stay where I am; for I am in a good position to observe the range, and watch the effect of the shot. I say, hadn't you better get behind the wood-pile again?"

"No, no," interrupted the Trapper; "the whole battery went at the word, Bill, and there isn't a gun or a gun-carriage left in the casement. Ye've wasted a gill of the yarb, and a quarter of a pound of the berry; and ye must hurry up with another outfit of bottles, or we'll have nothin' but water to drink at the dinner."

The dinner! That great event of the day, the crown and diadem to its royalty, and which became it so well, was ready promptly to the hour. The table, enlarged as it was to nearly double its original dimensions, could scarcely accommodate the abundance of the feast. Ah, if some sweet power would only enlarge our hearts when, on festive days, we enlarge our tables, how many of the world's poor, that now go hungry while we feast, would then be fed!

At one end of the table sat the Trapper, Wild Bill at the other. The woman's chair was at the center of one of the sides, so that she sat facing the fire, whose generous flames might well symbolize the abundance which amid cold and hunger had so suddenly come to her. On her right hand the two girls sat; on her left, the boy. A goodly table, a goodly fire, and a goodly company,—what more could the Angel of Christmas ask to see?

Thus were they seated, ready to begin the repast; but the

plates remained untouched, and the happy noises which had to
that moment filled the cabin ceased; for the Angel of Silence,
with noiseless step, had suddenly entered the room. There's a
silence of grief, there's a silence of hatred, there's a silence of
dread; of these, men may speak, and these they can describe.
But the silence of our happiness, who can describe that? When
the heart is full, when the long longing is suddenly met, when
love gives to love abundantly, when the soul lacketh nothing
and is content,— then language is useless, and the Angel of
Silence becomes our only adequate interpreter. A humble table,
surely, and humble folk around it; but not in the houses of the
rich or the palaces of kings does gratitude find her only home,
but in more lowly abodes and with lowly folk — ay, and often
at the scant table, too,— she sitteth a perpetual guest. Was it
memory? Did the Trapper at that brief moment visit his absent
friend? Did Wild Bill recall his wayward past? Were the
thoughts of the woman busy with sweet scenes of earlier days?
And did memory, by thus reminding them of the absent and
the past, of the sweet things that had been and were, stir
within their hearts thoughts of Him from whom all gifts de-
scend, and of His blessed Son, in whose honor the day was
named?

O Memory! thou tuneful bell that ringeth on forever, friend
at our feasts, and friend, too, let us call thee, at our burial,
what music can equal thine? For in thy mystic globe all tunes
abide, — the birthday note for kings, the marriage peal, the
funeral knell, the gleeful jingle of merry mirth, and those sweet

chimes that float our thoughts, like fragrant ships upon a fragrant sea, toward heaven, — all are thine! Ring on, thou tuneful bell; ring on, while these glad ears may drink thy melody; and when thy chimes are heard by me no more, ring loud and clear above my grave that peal which echoes to the heavens, and tells the world of immortality, that they who come to mourn may check their tears and say, "*Why do we weep? He liveth still!*"

"The Lord be praised fur His goodness!" said the Trapper, whose thoughts unconsciously broke into speech. "The Lord be praised fur His goodness, and make us grateful fur His past marcies, and the plenty that be here!" And looking down upon the viands spread before him he added, "The Lord be good to the boy, and make him as happy in his city home as be they who be wearin' and eatin' his gifts in the woods!"

"Amen!" said the woman softly, and a grateful tear fell on her plate.

"A—hem!" said Wild Bill; and then looking down upon his warm suit, he lifted his voice, and, bringing it out in a clear, strong tone, said, "*Amen! hit or miss!*"

At many a table that day more formal grace was said, by priest and layman alike, and at many a table, by lips of old and young, response was given to the benediction; but we doubt if over all the earth a more honest grace was said or more honestly assented to than the Lord heard from the cabin in the woods.

The feast and the merrymaking now began. The Old Trapper was in his best mood, and fairly bubbled over with humor.

The wit of Wild Bill was naturally keen, and it flashed at its best as he ate. The children stuffed and laughed as only children on such an elastic occasion can. And as for the poor woman, it was impossible for her, in the midst of such a scene, to be otherwise than happy, and she joined modestly in the conversation, and laughed heartily at the witty sallies.

But why should we strive to put on paper the wise, the funny, and the pleasant things that were said, the exclamations, the laughter, the story, the joke, the verbal thrust and parry of such an occasion? These, springing from the center of the circumstance, and flashed into being at the instant, cannot be preserved for after-rehearsal. Like the effervescence of champagne, they jet and are gone; their force passes away with the noise that accompanied its out-coming.

Is it not enough to record that the dinner was a success, that the Trapper's meats were put upon the table in a manner worthy of his reputation, that the woman's efforts at pastry-making were generously applauded, and that Wild Bill's tea and coffee were pronounced by the hostess the best she had ever tasted? Perhaps no meal was ever more enjoyed, as certainly none was ever more heartily eaten.

The wonder and pride of the table was the pudding,—a creation of Indian meal, flour, suet, and raisins, re-enforced and assisted by innumerable spicy elements supposed to be too mysterious to be grasped by the masculine mind. In the production of this wonderful centerpiece,—for it had been unanimously voted the place of honor,—the poor woman had summoned all the latent resources of her skill, and in reference to it her pride and fear contended, while the anxiety with which she rose to serve it was only too plainly depicted on her countenance. What if it should prove a failure? What if she had made a miscalculation as to the amount of suet required, — a point upon which she had been somewhat confused? What if the raisins were not sufficiently distributed? What if it wasn't done through, and should turn out pasty? Great Heavens! The last thought was of so overwhelming a character that no feminine courage could encounter it. Who may describe the look with which she watched the Trapper as he tasted it, or the expression of relief which brightened her anxious face when he pronounced warmly in its favor?

"It's a wonderful bit of cookin'," he said, addressing himself to Wild Bill, "and I sartinly doubt ef there be anythin' in the settlements to-day that can equal it. There be jest enough of the suet, and there be a plum for every mouthful; and it be solid enough to stay in the mouth ontil ye've had time to chew it, and git a taste of the corn, — and I wouldn't give a cent for a puddin' ef it gits away from yer teeth fast. Yis, it be a wonderful bit of cookin'," and, turning to the woman, he added, "ye may well be proud of it."

What higher praise could be bestowed? And as it was re-echoed by all present, and plate after plate was passed for a second filling, the dinner came to an end with the greatest good feeling and hilarity.

IV.

"Now fur the sled!" exclaimed the Trapper, as he rose from the table. "It be a good many years since I've straddled one, but nothin' settles a dinner quicker, or suits the leetle folks better. I conceit the crust be thick enough to bear us up, and, ef it is, we can fetch a course from the upper edge of the clearin' fifty rods into the lake. Come, childun, git on yer mittens and yer tippets, and h'ist along to the big pine, and ye shall have some fun ye won't forgit ontil yer heads be whiter than mine."

It is needless to record that the children hailed with delight the proposition of the Trapper, or that they were at the appointed spot long before the speaker and his companion reached it with the sled.

"Wild Bill," said the Trapper, as they stood on the crest of the slope down which they were to glide, "the crust be smooth as glass, and the hill be a steep un. I sartinly doubt ef mortal man ever rode faster than this sled'll be goin' by the time it gits to where the bank pitches into the lake ; and ef ye should git a leetle careless in yer steerin', Bill, and hit a stump, I conceit that nothin' but the help of the Lord or the rottenness of the stump would save ye from etarnity."

Now, Wild Bill was blessed with a sanguine temperament. To him no obstacle seemed serious if bravely faced. Indeed, his natural confidence in himself bordered on recklessness, to which the drinking habits of his life had, perhaps, contributed.

5

When the Trapper had finished speaking, Bill ran his eye carelessly down the steep hillside, smooth and shiny as polished steel, and said, "Oh, this isn't anything extry for a hill. I've steered a good many steeper ones, and in nights when the moon was at the half, and the sled overloaded at that. It don't make any difference how fast you go," he added, "if you only keep in the path, and don't hit anything."

"That's it, that's it," replied the Trapper. "But the trouble here be to keep in the path, fur, in the fust place, there isn't any path, and the stumps be pretty thick, and I doubt ef ye can line a trail from here to the bank by the lake without one or more sudden twists in it, and a twist in the trail, goin' as fast as we'll be goin', has got to be taken jediciously, or somethin' will happen. I say, Bill, what p'int will ye steer fur?"

Wild Bill, thus addressed, proceeded to give his opinion touching the proper direction of the flight they were to make. Indeed, he had been closely examining the ground while the Trapper was speaking, and therefore gave his opinion promptly and with confidence.

"Ye have chosen the course with jedgment," said the old man approvingly, after he had studied the line his companion pointed out critically for a moment. "Yis, Bill, ye have a nateral eye for the business, and I sartinly have more confidence in ye than I had a minit ago, when ye was talkin' about a steeper hill than this; fur this hill drops mighty sudden in the pitches, and the crust be smooth as ice, and the sled'll go like a streak when it gits started. But the course ye've p'inted out be a good un, fur there be only one bad turn in it, and good steerin' orter put a sled round that. I say," continued the old man, turning toward his companion, and pointing out the crook in the course at the bottom of the second dip, "can ye swing around that big stump there without upsettin', when ye come to it?"

"Swing around? Of course I can," retorted Wild Bill, positively. "There's plenty room to the left, and — "

"Ay, ay; there be plenty of room, as ye say, ef ye don't take too much of it," interrupted the Trapper. "But — "

"I tell you," broke in the other, "I'll turn my back to no man in steering a sled; and I can put this sled, and you on it, around that stump a hundred times, and never lift a runner."

"Well, well," responded the Trapper, "have it yer own way. I dare say ye be good at steerin', and I sartinly know I'm good at ridin'; and I can ride as fast as ye can steer, ef ye hit every stump in the clearin'. Now, childun," continued the old man, turning to the little group, "we be goin' to try the course; and ef the crust holds up, and Wild Bill keeps clear of the stumps, and nothin' onusual happens, ye shall have all the slidin' ye want afore ye go in. Come, Bill, git yer sled p'inted right, and I'll be gittin' on, and we'll see ef ye can steer an old man round a stump as handily as ye say ye can."

The directions of the Trapper were promptly obeyed, and in an instant the sled was in the right position, and the Trapper proceeded to seat himself with the carefulness of one who feels he is embarking on a somewhat uncertain venture, and has grave misgivings as to what will be the upshot of the undertaking. The sled was large and strongly built; and it added not a little to his comfort to feel that he could put entire confidence in the structure beneath them.

"The sled'll hold," he said to himself, "ef the loadin' goes to the jedgment."

The Trapper was no sooner seated than Wild Bill threw himself upon the sled, with one leg under him and the other stretched at full length behind. This was a method of steering that had come into vogue since the Trapper's boyhood, for in his day the steersman sat astride the sled, with his feet thrust forward, and steered by the pressure of either heel upon the snow.

"Hold on, Bill!" exclaimed the Trapper, whose eye this novel method of steering had not escaped. "Hold on, and hold up a minit. Heavens and 'arth! ye don't mean to steer this sled with one toe, do ye, and that, too, the length of a rifle-barrel astarn? Wheel round, and spread yer legs out as ye orter, and steer this sled in an honest fashion, or there'll be trouble aboard afore ye git to the bottom."

"Sit round!" retorted Bill. "How could I see to steer if I was sitting right back of you? For you're nigh a foot taller then I be, and your shoulders are as broad as the sled."

"Yer p'ints be well taken, fur sartin," replied the Trapper; "fur it be no more than reasonable that the man that steers should see where he be goin', and I am as anxious as ye be that ye should. Yis, I sartinly want ye to see where ye be goin' on this trip, anyhow, fur the crew be a fresh un, and the channel be a leetle crooked. But be ye sartin, Bill, that ye can fetch round that stump there as it orter be did, with nothin' but yer toe out behind? It may be the best way, as ye say, but it don't look like honest steerin' to a man of my years."

"I have used both ways," answered Bill, "and I give you my word, old man, that this is the best one. You can get a big swing with your foot stretched out in this fashion, and the sled feels the least pressure of the toe. Yes, it's all right. John Norton, are you ready?"

"Yis, yis, as ready as I ever shall be," answered the Trapper, in a voice in which doubt and resignation were equally mingled. "It may be as ye say," he continued; "but the rudder be too fur behind to suit me, and ef anything happens on this cruise, jest remember, Wild Bill, that my jedgment—"

The sentence the Trapper was uttering was abruptly cut short at this point; for Bill had started the sled with a sudden push, and leaped to his seat behind the Trapper as it glided downward and away. In an instant the sled was under full headway, for the dip was a sharp one, and the crust smooth as ice. Scarce had it gone ten rods from the point where it started before it was in full flight, and was gliding downward with what would have been, to any but a man of the steadiest nerve, a frightful velocity. But the Trapper was of too cool and courageous temperament to be disturbed even by actual danger. Indeed, the swiftness of their downward career, as the sled with a buzz and a roar swept along over the resounding crust, stirred the old man's blood with a tingle of excitement; while the splendid manner with which Wild Bill was keeping it to the course settled upon filled him with admiration, and was fast making him a convert to the new method of steering.

Downward they flashed. The Trapper's cap had been blown from his head; and as the old man sat bolt-upright on his sled, his feet bravely planted on the round, his face flushed, and his white hair streaming, he looked the very picture of hearty enjoyment. Above his head the face of Wild Bill looked actually sharpened by the pressure of the air on either cheek as it clove through it; but his lips were bravely set, and his eyes were fastened without winking on the big stump ahead, toward which they were rushing.

It was at this point that Wild Bill vindicated his ability as a steersman, and at the same time barely escaped shipwreck. At the proper moment he swept his foot to the left, and the sled, in obedience to the pressure, swooped in that direction. But in his anxiety to give the stump a wide berth, Bill overdid the pressure that was needed a trifle; for in calculating the curve required he had failed to allow for the sidewise motion of the sled, and, instead of hitting one stump, it looked for an instant as if he would be precipitated among a dozen.

"Heave her starn up, Wild Bill! up with her starn, I say," yelled the Trapper, "or there won't be a stump left in the clearin'."

With a quickness and courage that would have done credit to any steersman,— for the speed at which they were going

was terrific,— Bill swept his foot to the right, leaning his body
well over at the same instant. The Trapper instinctively sec-
onded his endeavors, and with hands that gripped either side
of the sled he hung over that side which was upon the point of
going into the air. For several rods the sled glided along on a
single runner, and then, righting itself with a lurch, jumped the
summit of the last dip, and raced away, like a swallow in full
flight, toward the lake.

Now, at the edge of the clearing that bounded the shore was
a bank of considerable size. Shrubs and stunted bushes fringed
the crest of it. These had been buried beneath the snow, and
the crust had formed smoothly over them ; and as it was upheld
by no stronger support than such as the hidden shrubbery fur-
nished, it was incapable of sustaining any considerable pressure.

Certainly no sled was ever moving faster than was Wild
Bill's when it came to this point; and certainly no sled ever
stopped quicker, for the treacherous crust dropped suddenly
under it, and the sled was left with nothing but the hind part
of one of the runners sticking up in sight. But though the sled
was suddenly checked in its career, the Trapper and Wild Bill
continued their flight. The former slid from the sled without
meeting any obstruction, and with the same velocity with which
he had been moving. Indeed, so little was his position changed,
that one might almost fancy that no accident had happened,
and that the old man was gliding forward to the end of the
course with an adequate structure under him. But with the
latter it was far different; for, as the sled stopped, he was pro-

jected sharply upward into the air, and, after turning several somersaults, he actually landed in front of the Trapper, and glided along on the slippery surface ahead of him. And so the two men shot onward, one after the other, while the children cackled from the hill-top, and the woman swung her bonnet over her head, and laughed from her position in the doorway.

"Bill," called the Trapper, when by dint of much effort they had managed to check their motion somewhat, "Bill, ef the cruise be about over, I conceit we'd better anchor hereabouts. But I shipped fur the voyage, and ye be capt'in, and as ye've finally got the right way to steer, I feel pretty safe techin' the futur'."

It was not until they had come to a full stop, and looked around them, that they realized the distance they had come; for they had in truth slid nearly across the bay.

"I've boated a good many times on these waters, and under sarcumstances that called fur 'arnest motion, but I sartinly never went across this bay as fast as I've did it to-day. How do ye feel, Bill, how do ye feel ?"

"A good deal shaken up," was the answer, "a good deal shaken up."

"I conceit as much," answered the Trapper, "I conceit as much, fur ye left the sled with mighty leetle deliberation; and when I saw yer legs comin' through the air, I sartinly doubted ef the ice would hold ye. But ye steered with jedgment; yis, ye steered with jedgment, Bill; and I'd said it ef we'd gone to the bottom."

The sun was already set when they returned to the cabin; for, selecting a safer course, they had given the children an hour's happy sliding. The woman had prepared some fresh tea and a lunch, which they ate with lessened appetites, but with humor that never flagged. When it was ended, the Old Trapper rose to depart, and with a dignity and tenderness peculiarly his own, thus spoke : —

"My good woman," he said, "the moon will soon be up, and the time has come fur me to be goin'. I've had a happy day with ye and the leetle uns; and the trail over the mountain will seem shorter, as the pups and me go home, thinkin' on't. Wild Bill will stay a few days, and put things a leetle more to rights, and git up a wood-pile that will keep ye from choppin' fur a good while. It's his own thought, and ye can thank him accordin'ly." Then, having kissed each of the children, and spoken a few words to Wild Bill, he took the woman's hand, and said : —

"The sorrers of life be many, but the Lord never forgits. I've lived until my head be whitenin', and I've noted that though He moves slowly, He fetches most things round about the time we need 'em; and the things that be late in comin', I conceit we shall git somewhere furder on. Ye didn't kill the big buck this mornin', but the meat ye needed hangs at yer door, nevertheless." And shaking the woman heartily by the hand, he whistled to the hounds, and passed out of the door. The inmates of the cabin stood and watched him, until, having climbed the slope of the clearing, he disappeared in the shadows of the forest; and then they closed the door. But more than once Wild Bill noted that as the woman stood wiping her dishes, she wiped her eyes as well; and more than once he heard her say softly to herself, "God bless the dear old man!"

Ay, ay, poor woman, we join thee in thy prayer. God bless the dear old man! and not only him, but all who do the deeds he did. God bless them one and all!

Over the crusted snow the Trapper held his course, until he came, with a happy heart, to his cabin. Soon a fire was burning on his own hearthstone, and the hounds were in their accustomed place. He drew the table in front, where the fire's fine light fell on his work, and, taking some green vines and branches from the basket, began to twine a wreath. One he twined, and then he began another; and often, as he twined the fadeless branches in, he paused, and long and lovingly looked at the two pictures hanging on the wall; and when the wreaths were twined, he hung them on the frames, and, standing in front of the dumb reminders of his absent ones, he said, "*I miss them so!*"

Ah! friend, dear friend, when life's glad day with you and me is passed, when the sweet Christmas chimes are rung for other ears than ours, when other hands set the green branches up, and other feet glide down the polished floor, may there be those still left behind to twine us wreaths, and say, "*We miss them so!*"

And this is the way John Norton the Trapper kept his Christmas.

THE MOUNTAIN TORRENT.

THE VAGABOND'S ROCK.

JOHN NORTON'S VAGABOND.

I.

A CABIN. A cabin in the woods. Of it I have written before, and of it I write again. The same great fireplace piled high with logs fiercely ablaze. Again on either side of the fireplace are the hounds gazing meditatively into the fire. The same big table, and on it the same great book, leather-bound and worn by the hands of many generations. And at the strong table, bending over the sacred book, with one huge finger marking a sentence, the same whitened head, the same man, large of limb and large of feature — John Norton, the Trapper.

"Yis, pups," said the Trapper, speaking to his dogs as one speaks to companions in council, "yis, pups, it must go in, for here it be writ in the Book — Rover, ye needn't have that detarmined look in yer eye — for here it be writ in the Book, I say, 'Do unto others as ye would that others should do unto you.'

"I know, old dog, that ye have seed me line the sights on the vagabonds, when ye and me have ketched 'em pilferin' the traps or tamperin' with the line, and I have trusted yer nose as often as my own eyes in trackin' the knaves when they'd got the start of us. And I will admit it, Rover, that the Lord gave ye a great gift in yer nose, so that ye be able to desarn the difference atween the scent of an honest trapper's moccasin and that of a vagabond. But that isn't to the p'int, Rover. The p'int is, Christmas be comin' and ye and me and Sport, yender, have sot it down that we're to have a dinner, and the question in council to-night is, Who shall we invite to our dinner? Here we have been arguin' the matter three nights atween us, pups, and we didn't git a foot ahead, and the reason that we didn't git a foot ahead was, because ye and me, Rover, naterally felt alike, for we have never consorted with vagabonds, and we couldn't bear the idee of invitin' 'em to this cabin and eatin' with 'em. So, ye and me agreed to-night we'd go to the Book and go by the Book, hit or miss. And the reason we should go to the Book and by the Book is, because, ef it wasn't for the Book, there wouldn't be any Christmas nor any Christmas dinner to invite anyone to, and so we went to the Book, and the Book says — I will read ye the words, Rover. And, Sport, though ye be a younger dog, and naterally of less jedgment, yit ye have yer gifts, and I have seed ye straighten out a trail that Rover and me couldn't ontangle. So do ye listen, both of ye, like honest dogs, while I read the words : —

"'Give to him that lacketh and from him that hath not withhold not thine hand.'

"There it be, Rover, — we are to give to the man that lacks, vagabond or no vagabond. Ef he lacks vict'als, we are to give him vict'als ; ef he lacks garments, we are to give him garments ; ef he lacks a Christmas dinner, Rover, we are to give him a Christmas dinner. But how are we to give him a Christmas dinner onless we give him an invite to it? For ye know yerself, Rover, that no vagabond would ever come to a cabin where ye and me be onless we axed him to.

"But there's another sentence here somewhere in the Book that bears on the p'int we be considerin'. '*When thou makest a dinner*'—that be exactly our case, Rover,—'*or a supper, call not thy friends, nor thy brethren, neither thy kinsmen, nor thy rich neighbors; lest they also bid thee again, and a recompense be made thee. But when thou makest a feast, call the poor, the maimed, the lame, the blind: and thou shalt be blessed; for they cannot recompense thee: for thou shalt be recompensed at the resurrection of the just.*'

"Furdermore, Rover, there's another passage that the lad, when he was on the 'arth, used to say each night afore he went to sleep, whether in the cabin or on the boughs. Sport, ye must remember it, for ye was his own dog. I am not sartin where it be writ in the Book, but that doesn't matter, for we all know the words,—it be from the great prayer,—'*Forgive us our trespasses as we forgive those who trespass against us,*' and the great prayer, as I conceit, is the only blazin' a man can trail by ef he hopes to fetch through to the Great Clearin' in peace.

"Now these vagabonds, Rover,—I needn't name 'em to ye,—have trespassed agin us; ye and me know it, for we've ketched 'em in their devilment, and, what is more to the p'int, the Lord knows it, too, for He's had His eye on 'em, and there's one up in the north country that wouldn't git an invite to this dinner, Bible or no Bible. But, barrin' this knave, who is beyend the range of our trails, there is not a single vagabond that has trespassed agin us that we mustn't forgive. For this be Christmas time, pups, and Christmas be a time for forgivin' and forgittin' all the evil that's been done agin us."

And here the old man paused and looked at the dogs and then gazed long and earnestly into the fire. To his face as he gazed came the look of satisfaction and a most placid peace. It was evident that if there had been a struggle between his natural feelings and his determination to celebrate the great Christmas festival in the true Christmas spirit the latter had won, and that the Christmas mood had at last entered into and possessed his soul. And after an interval he rose and carefully closing the great volume said : —

"And now, pups, as we've settled it atween us, and we all stand agreed in the matter, I'll git the bark and the coal, and we'll see how the decision of the council looks when it be put in writin'."

And in a moment the Trapper was again seated at the table with a large piece of birch bark in front of him and a hound on either side.

"I conceit, pups, that the letterin'," said the old man as he proceeded to sharpen the piece of charcoal he held in his hands, "should be of goodly size, for it may help some in readin', and I sartinly know it will help me in writin'."

With this honest confession of his lack of practice in penmanship, he proceeded to write : —

"*Any man or animil that be in want of vict'als or garments*

"Vagabonds included in this invite."

is invited to come on Christmas day—which be next week Thurs-
day—without furder axin', to John Norton's cabin, on Long Lake,
to eat Christmas dinner.   Vagabonds included in this invite."

"I can't say," said the Trapper, as he backed off a few paces
and looked at the writing critically, "I can't say that the
wordin' be exactly as the missioners would put it, and as for
the spellin', I haven't any more confidence in it than a rifle that
loads at the breech pin. The letterin' sartinly stands out well,
for the coal is a good un, and I put as much weight on it as I
thought it would bear, but there is sartinly a good deal of difference atween the ups and downs of the markin's, and the lines
slope off to'ard the northwest as ef they had started out to blaze
a trail through to St. Regis. That third line looks as ef it would
finally come together ef ye'd gin it time enough to git round
the circle, but the bark had a curve in it there, and the coal
followed the grain of the bark, and I am not to blame for that.
Rover, I more than half conceit by the look in yer eye that ye
see the difference in the size of them letters yerself. But ef ye
do ye be a wise dog to keep yer face steddy, for ef ye showed
yer feelin's, old as ye be, I'd edicate ye with the help of a moccasin."   And he looked at the old dog, whose face, as if he
realized the peril of his position, bore an expression of super-
natural gravity, with interrogative earnestness. "Never mind
the shape and size of the letters or the curve of the lines," he
added ; "the charcoal markin' stands out strong, and any hungry man with a leaky cabin for his home can sartinly study out
the words, and that's the chief p'int, as I understand it."

With this comforting reflection the Trapper made his preparations to retire for the night. He placed the skins for the dogs in the accustomed spot, lifted another huge log into the monstrous fireplace, swept the great hearthstone, bolted the heavy door, and then stretched himself upon his bed. But before he slept he gazed long and earnestly at the writing on the bark, and murmured: "'Vagabonds included in this invite.' Yis, the Book be right, Christmas be a day for forgivin' and forgittin'. And even a vagabond, ef he needs vict'als or garments or a right sperit, shall be welcome to my cabin." And then he slept.

In the vast and cheerless woods that night were some who were hungry and cold and wicked. What were Christmas and its cheer to them? What were gifts and giving, or who would spread for them a full table at which as guests of honor they might eat and be merry? And above the woods was a star leading men toward a manger, and a multitude of angels and an Eye that seeth forever the hungry and the cold and the wicked. On his bed slept the Trapper, with the look of the Christ on his face, and as he slept he murmured: —

"Yis, the Book be right: '*Let him who hath, give to them that hath not.*'" And above the woods, above the wicked and the cold, above the sleeping Trapper, and above the blessed words on the bark on his wall, above the spot where the Christ had thus received a forest incarnation, a great multitude of the heavenly host broke forth and sang: —

"*Glory to God in the highest, and on earth peace, good will toward men.*"

"And above the woods was a star."

II.

It was on the day before Christmas, and the sun was at its meridian. It was a day of brilliance and prophecy, and the prophecy which the Trapper read in the intense sky and vivid brightness of the sun's light told him of coming storm.

"Yis," muttered the old man, as he stood just outside the doorway of his cabin and carefully studied the signs of forest and sky, "yis, this is a weather breeder for sartin. I smell it in the air. The light is onnaterally bright and the woods onnaterally still. Snow will be flyin' afore another sunrise, and the woods will roar like the great lakes in a gale. I am sorry that it's comin', for some will be kept from the dinner. It's sartinly strange that the orderin' of the Lord is as it is, for a leetle more hurryin' and a leetle more stayin' on His part of the things that happen on the 'arth would make mortals a good deal happier, as I conceit."

Aye, aye, John Norton; a little more hurrying and a little more staying of things that happen on the earth would make mortals much happier. The great ship that is to-day a wreck would be sailing the sea, and the faces that stare ghastly white from its depths would be rosy with life's happy health. The flowers on her tomb would be twined in the bride's glossy hair, and the tower that now stands half builded would go on to its finishing. The dry fountain would still be in play and the leafless tree would stand green in its beauty and bloom. Who shall read us the riddle of the ordering in this world? Who shall

read the riddle, O man of whitened head, O woman whose life
is but a memory, who shall read us the Trapper's riddle, I say?

"There comes Wild Bill," exclaimed the Trapper joyfully,
"and one plate will have its eater for sartin." And the old
man laughed at the recollection of his companion's appetite.
"Lord-a-massy! that box on his sled is as big as the ark. I
wonder ef he has got a drove of animils in it."

Had the Trapper known the closeness of his guess as to the
contents of the huge box he would have marveled at his guess-
ing, for there certainly were animals in the box and of a sort
that usually are noisy enough and sure, at the least provocation,
to proclaim their name and nature.

But every animal, whether wild or domesticated, has its
habits, and many of the noisiest of mouths, when the mood is
on them, can be as dumb as a sphinx, and as Wild Bill came
shuffling up on his snowshoes, with a box of goodly size lashed
to his sled, not a sound proceeded therefrom. It is needless to
record that the greeting between the two men was most hearty.
How delightful is the meeting of men of the woods! Manly
are they in life and manly in their greeting.

"What have ye in the box, Bill?" queried the Trapper good-
naturedly. "It's big enough to hold a church bell, and a good
part of the steeple beside."

"It's a Christmas present for you, John Norton," replied Bill
gleefully. "You don't think I would come to your cabin to-day
and not bring a present, do you?"

"Gift or no gift, yer welcome would be the same," answered

the Trapper, "for yer heart and yer shootin' be both right, and ye will find the door of my cabin open at yer comin', whether ye come full handed or empty, sober or drunk, Wild Bill."

"I haven't touched a drop for twelve months," responded the other. "The pledge I gave you above the Christmas box in your cabin here last Christmas eve I have kept, and shall keep to the end, John Norton."

"I expected it of ye, yis, I sartinly expected it of ye, Bill, for ye came of good stock. Yer granther fit in the Revolution, and a man's word gits its value a good deal from his breedin', as I conceit," replied the Trapper. "But what have ye in the box,—bird, beast, or fish, Bill?"

"The trail runs this way," answered Bill. "I chopped a whole winter four year ago for a man who never paid me a cent for my work at the end of it. Last week I concluded to go and collect the bill myself, but not a thing could I get out of the knave but what's in the box. So I told him I'd take them and call the account settled, for I had read the writing on the bark you had nailed up on Indian Carry, and I said: 'They will help out at the dinner.'" And Bill proceeded to start one of the boards with his hatchet.

The Trapper, whose curiosity was now thoroughly excited, applied his eye to the opening, and as he did so there suddenly issued from the box the most unearthly noises, accompanied by such scratchings and clawings as could only have proceeded from animals of their nature under such extraordinary treatment as they had experienced.

"Heavens and 'arth!" exclaimed the Trapper, "ye have pigs in that box, Bill!"

"That's what I put in it," replied Bill, as he gave it another whack, "and that's what will come out of it if I can start the clinchings of these nails." And he bent himself with energy to his work.

"Hold up! Hold up, Bill!" cried the Trapper. "This isn't a bit of business ye can do in a hurry ef ye expect to git any profit out of the transaction. I can see only one of the pigs, but the one I can see is not over-burdened with fat, and it's agin reason to expect that he will be long in gittin' out when he starts, or wait for ye to scratch him when he breaks cover."

"Don't you be afraid of them pigs getting away from me, old man," rejoined Bill, as he pried away at the nails. "I don't expect that the one that starts will be as slow as a funeral when he makes his first jump, but he won't be the only pig I've caught by the leg when he was two feet above the earth."

"Go slow, I say, go slow!" cried the Trapper, now thoroughly alarmed at the reckless precipitancy of his companion; "the pigs, as I can see, belong to a lively breed, and it is sheer foolishness to risk a whole winter's choppin'—"

Not another word of warning did the Old Trapper utter, for suddenly the nails yielded, the board flew upward, and out of the box shot a pig. It is in the interest of accurate statement and everlasting proof of Wild Bill's alertness to affirm and record that the flying pig had taken only two jumps before his owner was atop of him, and both disappeared over the bank in a whirlwind of flying snow. Nor had the Trapper been less dexterous, for no sooner had the sandy colored streak shot through the hole made by the hatchet of the man who had sledded him forty miles that he might present him to the Trapper as a contribution to the Christmas dinner, than the old man dropped himself on to the box, thereby effectually barring the exit of the other porcine sprinter.

"Get your gun, get your gun, Old Trapper!" yelled Bill from the whirlwind of snow. "Get your gun, I say, for this infernal pig is getting the best of me."

"I can't do it, Bill," cried the Trapper; "I can't do it. I am doin' picket duty on the top of this box, with a big hole under me and another pig under the hole."

At the same instant the pig and Wild Bill shot up the bank into full view. Bill had lost his grip on the leg, but had made good his hold on an ear, and had the Trapper been a betting man, it is doubtful if he would have placed money on either. Had he done so, the odds would have been slightly in favor of the pig.

"Hold on to him, Bill!" cried the Trapper, laughing at the spectacle in front of him till the tears stood in his eyes. "Hold on to him, I say. Remember, ye have three months of chop-pin' in yer grip; the pig under me is gittin' lively, and the prof-its of the other three months be onsartin. O Lord!" ejaculated the old man, partially sobered at the prospect, "here comes the pups and the devil himself will now be to pay!"

The anxiety and alarming prediction of the Trapper were in

the next instant fully justified, for the two dogs, unaccustomed
to the scent and cries of the animals, but thoroughly aroused
at the noise and fury of the contest, came tearing down the
slope through the snow at full speed. The pig saw them coming and headed for the southern angle of the cabin, with Bill
streaming along at his side. In an instant he reappeared at
the northern corner, with Bill still fastened to his ear and the
hounds in full cry just one jump behind him. It is not an accurate statement to say that Wild Bill was running beside the
pig, for his stride was so elongated that when one of his feet
left the ground it was impossible to predict when or where it
would strike the earth, or whether it would ever strike again.
The two flying objects, as they came careering down the slope
directly toward the Trapper, who was heroically holding himself
above the aperture in the box with the porcine volcano in full
play under him, presented the dreadful appearance of Biela's
comet when, rent by some awful explosion, the one half was on
the point of taking its eternal farewell of the other.

"Lift the muzzle of yer piece, Wild Bill!" yelled the Trapper. "Lift the muzzle, I say, and allow three feet for windage,
or ye'll make me the bull's-eye for yer pig!"

The advice, or rather, let us say, the expostulation of the
Trapper, was the best which, under the circumstances, could be
given, but no directions, however correct, might prevent the
dreadful catastrophe. The old man stuck heroically to his post,
and the pig stuck with equal pertinacity to his course. He
struck the box on which the Trapper sat with the force of a

stone from a catapult, and dogs, men, and pigs disappeared in
the snow.

When the Trapper had wiped the snow from his eyes, the
spectacle that he beheld was, to say the least, extraordinary.
The head of one dog was in sight above the snow, and nigh the
head he could make out the hind legs and tail of another. In
an instant Wild Bill's cap came in sight, and from under it a
series of sounds was coming as if he were talking earnestly to
himself, while far down the trail leading to the river he caught
the glimpse of two sandy-colored objects going at a speed to
which matter can only attain when it has become permanently
detached from this earth and superior to the laws of gravita-
tion.

For several minutes not a word was said. The catastrophe
had been so overwhelming and the wreck of Bill's hopes so
complete that it made speech on his part impossible. The Trapper, from a fine sense of feeling and regard for his companion,
remained silent, and the dogs, uncertain as to what was expected of them, kept their places in the snow. At last the old
man struggled to his feet and silently started toward the cabin.
Wild Bill followed in equal silence, and the dogs as mutely
brought up the rear. The depressed, not to say woe-begone,
appearance of the singular procession certainly had in it, in the
fullest measure, all the elements of humor. In this suggestive
manner the column filed into the cabin. The dogs stole softly
to their accustomed places, Wild Bill dropped into a chair, and
the Trapper addressed himself mechanically to some domestic

concerns. At last the silence became oppressive. Wild Bill turned in his chair, and, facing the Trapper, said : —

"It's too devilish bad ! "

"Ef ye was in council, ginerals or privits, ye'd carry every vote with ye on that statement, Bill," said the Trapper with deliberation.

"Do you think there is any chance, old man ?" queried Bill, earnestly.

"Not on the 'arth, Bill," answered the Trapper. "Ye see," he continued, "the snow wasn't so deep on my side the trail and I had my eye on them pigs afore ye got yer head above the drift, and I noted the rate of their movin'. They was goin' mighty fast, Bill, mighty fast. Ye must take into account that they had the slope in their favor and sartin experiences behind. I've sighted on a good many things that was gifted in runnin' and flyin', and I never kept a bullit in the barrel when I wanted feather, fur, or meat, because of the swiftness of the motion, but ef I had ben standin' ten rods from that trail and loved the meat like a settler, I wouldn't have wasted powder or lead on them pigs, Bill." And the two men, looking into each other's faces, laughed like boys.

"Where do you think they'll fetch up, John Norton ?" queried Bill, at last.

"They won't fetch up," replied the Trapper, wiping his eyes, "leastwise not this year. Henry has told me that it is twenty-four thousand miles around the 'arth, and it looked to me as ef them pigs had started out to sarcumnavigate it, and I conceit

it'll be about a month afore they will come through this clearin'
agin. I may be a little amiss in my calkerlatin', but a day more
or less won't make any difference with you and me, nor with
the pigs, either, Bill. They may be a trifle leaner when they
pass the cabin next time, but their gait will be jest the same, as
I conceit." And after a moment, he asked, sympathetically :—

"How far did ye sled them pigs, Bill ?"

"Forty mile," answered Bill, dejectedly.

"It's a goodly distance, considerin' the natur' of the animils," replied the Trapper, "and ye must have been tempted to
onload the sled more'n once, Bill."

"I would have unloaded it," responded the other, "I would
have unloaded the cussed things more than once, but I had
nothing else to bring you, and I thought they'd look mighty
fine standing up on the table with an apple in each mouth and
their tails curled up, as I've seen them at the barbecues."

"So they would, so they would, Bill ; but ye never could have
kept 'em on the table. No amount of cookin' would have ever
taken the speed out of them pigs. Ef ye had nailed 'em to the
table they'd have taken the table and cabin with 'em. It's better as it is, Bill ; so cheer up and we'll git at the cookin'. "

Cooking is more than an art ; it is a gift. Genius, and genius alone, can prepare a feast fit for the feaster. Woe be to the
wretch who sees nothing in preparing food for the mouth of
man save manual labor. Such a knave should be basted on his
own spit. An artist in eating can alone appreciate an artist in

cooking. When food is well prepared it delights the eye, it intoxicates the nose, it pleases the tongue, it stimulates the appetite, and prolongs the healthy craving which it finally satisfies, even as the song of the mother charms the child which it gradually composes for slumber.

The Old Trapper was a man of gifts and among his gifts was that of cooking. For sixty years he had been his own *chef*, with a continent for his larder, and to more than one gourmand of the great cities the tastiness and delicacy of his dishes had been a revelation — more than one epicure of the clubs had gone from his cabin not only with a full but a surprised stomach.

It is easy to imagine the happiness that this host of the woods experienced in preparing the feast for the morrow. He entered upon his labors, whose culmination was to be the great event of the year, with the alacrity of one who had mentally discussed and decided every point in anticipation. There was no cause for haste, and hence there was no confusion. He could not foretell the number of his guests, but this did in no way disconcert him. He had already decided that no matter how many might come there should be enough. In Wild Bill he had an able and willing assistant, and all through the afternoon and well into the evening the two men pushed on the preparation for the great dinner.

The large table, constructed of strong maple plank, was sanded and scoured until it shone almost snowy white. On it was placed a buck, roasted a la barbecue, the skin and head skillfully reconnected with the body and posed, muzzle lifted, antlers laid well

back, head turned, ears alert, as he stood in the bush when the
Trapper's bullet cut him down. At one end of the table a bear's
cub was in the act of climbing a small tree, while at the other
end a wild goose hung in mid-air, suspended by a fine wire from
the ceiling, with neck extended, wings spread, legs streaming
backward, as he looked when he drove downward toward open
water to his last feeding.

The great cabin was a bower of beauty and fragrance. The
pungent odor of gummy boughs and of bark, under which still
lurked the amber-colored sweat of heated days and sweltering
nights, pervaded it. On one side of the cabin hung a huge piece of
white cotton cloth, on which the Trapper, with a vast outlay of
patience, had stitched small cones of the pine into the conven-
tional phrase,

"A MERRY CHRISTMAS TO YE ALL."

"It must have taken you a good many evenings to have done
that job," said Wild Bill, pointing with the ladle he held in
his hand toward the illuminated bit of sheeting.

"It did, Bill, it did," replied the Trapper, "and a solemn and
a lively time I had of it, for I hadn't but six big needles in the
cabin and I broke five on 'em the fust night, for the cones was
gummy and hard, and it takes a good, stiff needle to go
through one ef the man who is punchin' it through hasn't any
thimble and the ball of his thumb is bleedin'. Lord-a-massy,
Bill, Rover knew the trouble I was havin' as well as I did, for
arter I had broken the second needle and talked about it a
moment, the old dog got oneasy and began to edge away, and

by the time I had broken the fourth needle and got through washin' my thumb he had backed clean across the cabin and sat jammed up in the corner out there flatter than a shingle."

"And what did he do when the fifth needle broke?" queried Bill, as he thrust his ladle into the pot.

"Heavens and 'arth, Bill, why do ye ax sech foolish questions? Ye know it wasn't a minit arter that fifth needle broke, leavin' the bigger half stickin' under the nail of my forefinger, afore both of the pups was goin' out through the door there as ef the devil was arter 'em with a fryin' pan, and a chair a leetle behind him. But a man can't stand everything, ef he be a Christian man and workin' away to git a Christmas sign ready; can he, Bill?"

It is in harmony with the facts of the case for me to record that Wild Bill never answered the Old Trapper's very proper interrogation, but sat down on the floor and thrust his legs up in the air and yelled, and after the spasm left him he got up slowly, sat down in a chair, and looked at the Trapper with wet eyes and mouth wide open.

The Old Trapper evidently relished the mirthfulness of his companion, for his face was lighted with the amused expression of the humorist when he has told to an appreciative comrade an experience against himself. But in an instant his countenance dropped, and, looking at the huge kettle that stood half buried in the coals and warm ashes in front of the glowing logs and into which Bill had been so determinedly thrusting his ladle only a moment before, he exclaimed : —

"Bill, I have lost all confidence in yer cookin' abilities. Ye said that ye knew the natur' of corn meal and that ye could fill a puddin' bag jediciously, and though it isn't ten minits sence ye tied the string and the meal isn't half swollen yit, yer whole bag there is on the p'int of comin' out of the pot."

At this alarming announcement Wild Bill jumped for the fireplace and in an instant he had placed the spade-shaped end of his ladle, whose handle was full three feet long, at the very center of the lid that was already lifted two inches from the rim of the kettle, and was putting a good deal of pressure upon it. Confident in his ability to resist any further upward tendency, and to escape the threatened catastrophe, he coolly replied:—

"It strikes me that you are a good deal excited over a little matter, old man. The meal has got through swelling—"

"No, it hasn't, no, it hasn't," returned the Trapper. "Half the karnels haven't felt the warmin' of the hot water yit, and I can see that the old lid is liftin'."

"No, it isn't lifting, either, John Norton," returned Wild Bill determinedly; "and it won't lift unless the shaft of this ladle snaps."

"The ladle be a good un," returned the Trapper, now fully assured that no human power could avert the coming catastrophe, and keenly enjoying his companion's extremity and the humor of the situation. "The ladle be a good un, for I fashioned it from an old paddle of second growth ash, whose blade I had twisted in the rapids, and ye can put yer whole weight on it."

"Old man," cried Bill, now thoroughly alarmed, "the lid is lifting."

"Sartinly, sartinly," returned the Trapper. "It's lifted fully half an inch sence ye placed yer ladle to it, and it'll keep on liftin'. Rover knows what is comin' as well as I do, for the old dog, as ye see, begins to edge away, and Sport has started for the door already."

"What shall I do, John Norton? What shall I do? The lid is lifting again."

"Is yer ladle well placed, Bill? Have ye got it in the center of the lid?" returned the Trapper.

"Dead in the center, old man," responded Bill, confidently, "dead in the center."

"Put yer whole weight on it, then, and don't waste yer strength in talkin'. Ye know yer own strength, and I know the strength of Indian meal when hot water gits at it, and ef the ladle don't slip or the kettle-lid split it's about nip and tuck atween ye."

"Old man," yelled Bill, as he put his whole weight on the ladle handle, "this lid has lifted again. Get a stick and come here and help me."

"No, no, Bill," answered the Trapper, "the puddin' is of yer own mixin' and ye must attend to the job yerself. I stuck to yer box with a hole underneath me and a pig under the hole till somethin' happened and ye must stick to yer puddin'."

"But I can't hold it down, John Norton," yelled poor Bill. "The lid has lifted again and the whole darned thing is coming out of the pot."

"I conceit as much, I conceit as much," answered the Trapper. "There go the pups out of the door, Bill, and when the dogs quit the cabin it's time for the master to foller." And the old man started for the door.

The catastrophe! Who could describe it? Bill's strength was adequate, but no human power could save the pudding. Even as Bill put his strength on to the ladle, the wooden cover of the kettle split with a sharp concussion in the middle, the kettle was upset, and poor Bill, covered with ashes and pursued by a cloud of steam, shot out of the door and plunged into the snow.

Oh, laughter, sweet laughter, laugh on and laugh ever! In the smile of the babe thou comest from heaven. In the girl's rosy dimples, in the boy's noisy glee, in the humor of strong men, and the wit of sweet women, thou art seen as a joy and a comfort to us humans. When fortune deserts and friends fall away, he who keeps thee keeps solace and health, hope and heart, in his bosom. When the head groweth white and the eye getteth dim, and the soul goeth out through the slow closing gates of the senses, be thou then in us and of us, thou sweet angel of heaven, that the smile of the babe in its first happy sleep may come back to our faces as we lie at the gates in our last and — perhaps — most peaceful slumber!

The laughter and the labor of the day were ended. The work of preparation for the dinner on the morrow had extended well into the evening, and at its conclusion the two men, satisfied with the result of the pleasant task and healthily weary, retired

to their cots. It is needless to say that the thoughts of each
were happy and their feelings peaceful, and to such slumber
comes quickly. Outside the world was white and still, with the
stillness that precedes the coming of a winter storm. Through
the voiceless darkness a few feathery prophecies of coming snow
were settling lazily downward. The great stones in the fireplace
were still white with heat, and the cabin was filled with the
warm afterglow of burned logs and massive brands that ever and
anon broke apart and flamed anew.

Suddenly the Trapper lifted himself on his couch, and, looking over toward his companion, said : —

"Bill, didn't ye hear the bells ring ? "

Wild Bill lifted himself to his elbow, and in sheer astonishment stared at the Trapper, for he well knew there wasn't a
bell within fifty miles. The old man noticed the astonishment
of his companion and, realizing the incredibility of the supposi-
tion, said as if in explanation of the strangeness of his question-
ing : —

"This be the night on which memory takes the home trail,
Bill, and the thoughts of the aged go backward." And, laying
his head again on the pillow, he murmured : "I sartinly conceited I heerd the bells ringin'." And then he slept.

Aye, aye, Old Trapper ; we of whitening heads know the
truth of thy saying and thy dreaming. Thou didst hear the bells
ring. For often as we sleep on Christmas eve the ringing of
bells comes to us. Marriage peal and funeral knell, chimes and
tolling, clash of summons and measured stroke, dying noises

"Where be the ships?"

from a dead past swelling and sinking, sinking and swelling, like falling and failing surf on a wreck-strewn beach. Ah, me! where be the ships, the proud, white-sailed ships, the rich-laden ships, whose broken timbers and splintered spars lie now dank, weed-grown, sand-covered, on that sorrowful shore, on that mournfully resounding shore of our past?

But other bells, thank God, sound for us all, Old Trapper, on Christmas eve,—not the bells of the past, but the bells of the future. And they ring loud and clear, and they will ring forever, for they are swung by the angels of God. And they tell of a new life, a new chance, and a new opportunity for us all.

Morning dawned. The day verified the Trapper's prophecy, for it came with storm. The mountain back of the cabin roared as if aërial surf was breaking against it. The air was thick with snow that streamed, whirled, and eddied through it dry and light as feathers of down.

"Never mind the storm, Bill," said the Trapper cheerily, as he pushed the door open in the gray dawn and looked out into the maze of whirling, rushing snowflakes. "A few may be hindered, and one or two fetch through a leetle late, but there'll be an 'arnest movement of teeth when the hour for eatin' comes and the plates be well filled."

Dinner was called prompt to the hour, and again was the old man's prediction realized. The table lacked not guests, for nearly every chair was occupied. Twenty men had breasted the storm that they might be at that dinner, and some had traversed

a thirty mile trail that they might honor the old man and share
his generous cheer. It was a remarkable and, perhaps we may
say, a motley company that the Trapper looked upon as he took
his place, knife and fork in hand, at the head of the table, with
a hound on either side of his great chair, to perform the duty
of host and chief carver.

"Friends," said the Trapper, standing erect in his place and
looking cheerfully at the row of bearded and expectant faces
on either hand in front of him, "friends, I axed ye to come
and eat this Christmas dinner with me because I love the com-
panionship of the woods and hated, on this day of human feastin'
and gladness, to eat my food alone. I also conceited that some
of ye felt as I did, and that the day would be happier ef we
spent it together. I knew, furdermore, that some of ye were
not born in the woods, but were newcomers, driven here as a
canoe to a beach in a gale, and that the day might be long and
lonesome to ye ef ye had to stay in yer cabins from mornin' till
night alone by yerselves. And I also conceited that here and
there might be a man who had been onfortunit in his trappin'
or his venturs in the settlements, and might act'ally be in need
of food and garments, or it may be he had acted wickedly at
times, and had lost confidence in his own goodness and the
goodness of others, and I said I will make the tarms of the invitin' broad enough to include each and all, whoever and whatever he may be.

"And now, friends," continued the old man, "I be glad to
see ye at my table, and I hope ye have brought a good appetite

with ye, for the vic'tals be plenty and no one need scrimp the
size of his eatin'. Let us all eat heartily and be merry, for this
be Christmas. Ef we've had bad luck in the past we'll hope for
better luck in the futur' and take heart. Ef we've been heavy-
hearted or sorrowful we will chirk up. Ef any have wronged
us we will forgive and forgit. For this be Christmas, friends,
and Christmas be a day for forgivin' and forgittin.' And now,
then," continued the old man, as he flourished his knife and
grasped the huge fork preparatory to plunging it into the venison haunch in front of him, "with good appetites and a cheer-
ful mind let us all fall to eatin'."

III.

THUS went the feasting. Hunger had brought its appetite to
the plentiful table, and the well cooked viands provoked its in-
dulgence. If the past of any of the Trapper's guests had been
sorrowful, the unhappiness of it for the moment was forgotten.
Stories crisp as snow-crust and edged with aptness, happy
memories and reminiscences of frolic and fun, sly hits and keen
retorts, jokes and laughter, rollicked around the table and shook
it with mirthful explosions. The merriment was at its height
when a loud summons sounded upon the door. It was so im-
perious as well as so unexpected that every noise was instantly
hushed, and every face at the table was turned in surprise to
wait the entrance.

"Come in," cried the Trapper, cheerily; "whoever ye be, ye
be welcome ef ye be a leetle late."

The response of him who so emphatically sought admission to the feast was as prompt as his summons had been determined. For, without an instant's delay or the least hesitancy of movement, the great door was pushed suddenly inward and a man stepped into the room.

A sturdy fellow he was, swarth of skin and full whiskered. His hair was black and coarse and grown to his shoulders. His eyes were black as night, largely orbed under heavy brows, not lacking a certain wicked splendor. His face was strongly featured and stamped in every line and curve and prominence with the impress of unmistakable power. In his right hand he carried a rifle, and in his left a bundle, snugly packed and protected from the storm in wrappings of oiled cloth. The strong light, into the circle of which he had so suddenly stepped, blinded him for a moment, while to those who sat staring at him it brought out with vivid distinctiveness every feature of his strong and, save for a certain hardness of expression, handsome face. It was evident that the man, whoever he was and whatever he might be, was under the pressure of some impulse or conviction which had urged him on to the Trapper's cabin and the Trapper's presence. For, no sooner had he closed the door and shaken the snow, with which he was covered, from his garments, than, regardless of those who sat staring in startled interrogation at him, he strode to the head of the table where the Old Trapper sat, and, looking him straight in the face, said : —

"Do you know who I am, John Norton?"

"Sartinly," answered the Trapper, "ye be Shanty Jim, and ye have camped these three year and more at the outlet of Bog Lake."

"Do you know that I am a thief, and a sneak thief at that?" continued the newcomer, speaking with a fierce directness that was startling.

"I've conceited ye was," answered the Trapper, calmly.

"Do you know it, know it to a certainty?" and the words came out of his mouth like the thrust of a knife.

"Yis, I know that ye be a thief, Shanty Jim," replied the Trapper, "know it to a sartinty."

"Do you know that I have stolen skins from you, old man, skins and traps both?" continued the other.

"I laid in ambush for ye once at the falls of Bog River, and I seed ye take an otter from a trap that I sot," replied the Trapper.

"Why didn't you shoot me when I stood skin in hand?" queried the self-confessed thief.

"I can't tell ye," answered the Trapper, "fer my eye was at the sights and my finger on the trigger, and the feelin' of natur' was strong within me to crop one of yer ears then and there, Shanty Jim, but somethin', mayhap the sperit of the Lord, staid my finger, and ye went with yer thievin' in yer hand to yer camp ontetched and onhindered."

"Do you know what brought me to this cabin and to your presence — the presence of the man whose skins and whose traps I have stolen — and made me confess to his face and before these men here that I am a thief and a scoundrel; do you know what brought me here, a miserable cuss that I am and have been for years, John Norton?" And the man's speech was the speech of one who had been educated to use words rightly and was marked with intense, even dramatic, earnestness.

"I can't conceit, onless the sperit of the Lord."

"The spirit of the Lord had nothing to do with it," interrupted the other fiercely. "If there is any such influence at work in this world as the preachers tell of, why has it not prevented me from being a thief? Why did it not prevent me from doing what I did and being what I was in my youth,— me, whose mother was an angel and whose father was a patriarch? No, it was nothing under God's heavens, old man, but your invitation scrawled with a coal on a bit of birch bark inviting anyone in these woods who needed victuals and clothes and a right spirit to come to your cabin on Christmas day; and had you written nothing else I would not have cared a cuss for it or for you, but you did write something else, and it was this: 'Vagabonds included in this invite.'

"When I read that, old man, my breath left me and I stood and stared at the letters on that bark as a devil might gaze at a pardon signed with the seal manual of the Almighty, for in my hand was a trap that bore the stamp 'J. N.' and the skin of an otter I had taken from the trap. And there I stood, a thief and a scoundrel, with your property in my hands and read your invitation to all the needy in the woods to come to your cabin on Christmas day and that vagabonds were included."

"That meant you, by thunder!" exclaimed Wild Bill.

"Yes, it did mean me," returned Shanty Jim, "and I knew it. Standing there in the snow with the stolen skin and trap in my hand, I realized what I was and what John Norton was and the difference between him and myself and most of the world. I went to the tree to which the bark that bore the blessed letters was nailed; I took it down from the tree; I placed it next my bosom and buttoned my coat above it and, thus resting upon my heart, I bore it to my shanty."

"It was as good as a Bible to you," said Wild Bill.

"A Bible!" rejoined the man with emphasis. "Better than all Bibles. Better than churches and preachers, better than formal texts and utterances, for that bit of bark told me of a man here in the woods good enough and big enough to forgive and forget. All that night I sat and gazed at that piece of bark and the writing on it, and as I gazed my heart melted within me. For there it was ever before my eyes — 'Vagabonds included in this invite.' 'Vagabonds included in this invite.' And finally the words passed into the air, and wherever I looked I saw, 'Vagabonds included in this invite.'"

"Yis, them be the very words I writ," said the Trapper, gravely.

"And I saw more than the words written on the bark, John Norton," resumed the man. "For looking at it I saw all my past life and the evil of it and what a scoundrel I had become; my eyes saw with a new sight, and I said, when the sun comes I will rise and go to the man who wrote those words and tell

him what they did for me. And here I am, a vagabond who
has accepted your invitation to spend Christmas with you, and
here in this pack are the skins and the traps I have stolen
from you, and I ask your forgiveness and that you will take my
hand in proof of it, that I may come to your table feeling that
I am a man, and a vagabond no longer."

"Heart and hand be yours now and forever, Shanty Jim,"
cried the Trapper, joyfully; and, rising from his chair, he met
the outstretched hand of the repentant vagabond with his own
hearty grasp. "And may the Lord be with ye ever more."

"Amen!" It was Wild Bill, the once drunkard, who said the
sweet word of prayer and assent, and he said it softly. And
that murmur of amen and amen went round the great table
like the murmur of prayer and of praise. And then it passed
out and rose up from the cabin, and the air in its joy passed it
on, and the stars took it up and thrilled it around their vast
courses of glorified light, and through the high heavens it sang
itself onward from order to order of angels until it reached Him
whom no man hath seen or may ever see, in all and over all,
God! blessed forever!

Has Nature knowledge? Is she conscious of the evil and the
good among men, and has she a heart that saddens at their sorrow and rejoices in their joy? Perhaps. For, suddenly, even as
the two men joined their hands, the fury of the storm checked
itself, and a stillness — the stillness of a great calm — fell on
the woods, and through the sudden, the unexpected, the blessed
stillness, to the ears of one of the two men — yea, to him who

had forgiven — there came the melody of bells swinging slowly
and softly to and fro.

Oh, bells, invisible bells! Bells of the soul, bells high in
heaven, swing softly, swing low, swing sweet, and swing ever
for us, one and all, when we at our tables sit feasting. Swing
for us living, swing for us dying, and may the cause of your
swinging be our forgiving and forgetting.

"John Norton," said the man, "you have called me Shanty
Jim, and that is well, for in the woods here that is my name,
but in the city where I lived and whence I fled, fled because of
my misdeeds, years ago, I have another name, a name of power
and wealth and honor for more than two centuries. There I
have a home, and in that home to-night sits my aged father
and white-haired mother. I am going back to them clothed and
in my right mind. Think of it, Old Trapper, going back to my
home, my boyhood's home, to my father and my mother. All
day as I tramped on the trail toward your cabin, my mind has
been filled with memories of the past, and the words of a sweet
old song I used to sing when too young to feel the tenderness
of it, have been ringing in my ears."

"Sing us the song, sing us the song!" cried Wild Bill, and
every man at the table cried with him, "Sing us the song!"

"Aye, aye," assented the Trapper, "sing us the song, Shanty
Jim; we be men of the woods at this table, and some of us
have had losses and sorrers, and all of us have memories of
happy days that be gone. Stand here by my side and sing us
the song that has been ringin' in yer ears all day. This is a

table of feastin', and feastin' means more than eatin'. Sing us the song that tells ye of the past, of yer boyhood's days and father and mother."

Oh, the secrets of the woods! How many have fled to them for concealment and refuge! In them piety has built its retreat, learning has sought retirement, broken pride a mask, and misfortune a haven. And in response to the Trapper's invitation there had come to his cabin and were now grouped about his table more of ability, more of knowledge, more of struggle and failure, and more of reminiscence than might be found, perhaps, in the same number of guests at any other table on that Christmas day in the world.

Never did singer sing sweeter or more touching song, or to more receptive company.

> " Backward, turn backward, oh, Time, in your flight,
> Make me a child again just for to-night.
> Mother, come back from the echoless shore,
> Take me again to your heart, as of yore ;
> Kiss from my forehead the furrows of care,
> Smooth the few silver threads out of my hair,
> Over my slumbers your loving watch keep ; —
> Rock me to sleep, mother, rock me to sleep.

> CHORUS :—" Clasped to your heart in a loving embrace,
> With your light lashes just sweeping my face,
> Never hereafter to wake or to weep ; —
> Rock me to sleep, mother, rock me to sleep.

"Over my heart, in the days that are flown,
No love like mother-love ever has shone;
No other worship abides and endures,
Faithful, unselfish, and patient like yours;
None like a mother can charm away pain
From the sick soul and the world-weary brain.
Slumber's soft calms o'er my heavy lids creep; —
Rock me to sleep, mother, rock me to sleep.

    CHORUS.—

"Come, let your brown hair, just lighted with gold,
Fall on your shoulders again, as of old;
Let it drop over my forehead to-night,
Shading my faint eyes away from the light;
For with its sunny-edged shadows once more,
Haply, will throng the sweet visions of yore;
Lovingly, softly, its bright billows sweep; —
Rock me to sleep, mother, rock me to sleep."

    CHORUS.—

Never was the sweet and touching song sung under more suggestive circumstances, and never was it received into more receptive hearts. The voice of the repentant vagabond was of the finest quality, a pure, resonant tenor, and, through the splendid avenue of expression which the words and music of the song made for his emotions, he poured his soul forth without restraint. The effect of his effort was what would be expected when the character of the audience and the occasion is considered. Many an eye was wet with tears, and the voices that took up the refrain here and there trembled with emotion.

The Old Trapper, himself, was not unmoved, for, as the song closed, after a few moments of silence, he said :—

"Ye sang the song well, Shanty Jim, and many be the memories it has stirred in the breasts of us all. May yer home-comin' be as happy as was the boy's we read of in the Scriptur', although I never could conceit why the mother was not there to go forth to meet him, and fall on his neck with the father, and ef I'd had the writin' of it I'd had the mother git to him a leetle fust, and hers the fust arms that was thrown round his neck, for that would be more nateral, as I conceit. And I sartinly trust, as do all of us here, that ye will find mother and father both waitin' and watchin' for ye when the curve of the trail brings ye in the sight of the cabin. And ye sartinly will take with ye the good wishes of us all. Come, take the chair here by my side, and we will all talk as we eat; aye, and sing, too, for this be Christmas, and Christmas be the time for eatin' and singin', but, above all else, for forgivin' and forgittin'." At the word the happy feasters went on with the feasting.

Long and merry was the meal. As the hours passed the eating ceased, and the feast of reason and the flow of soul began. Memories of other days were recalled, confessions made, sorrow for misdoings felt and spoken, and, gradually growing, as grows the light of dawn, a fine atmosphere of hope, charity, and courage spread from heart to heart, until at last it filled with its genial and illuminating presence every bosom. In such a mood on the part of the host and guests alike the feast came to its close. His Christmas dinner had been all that the Old Trapper had hoped, and his heart was filled with happiness. He rose from his chair, and, standing erect in his place, said : —

"Ye tell me that the time has come for ye to go, and I dare say ye be right, but I be sorry we must part, for in partin' we be never sure of a meetin', and, therefore, as I conceit, all the partin's on the 'arth be more or less sad, but all parted trails, it may be, will come together in the eend. But afore ye go I want to thank ye for comin', and I hope ye will all come agin, and whenever yer needs or yer feelin's incline ye this way. One thing I want to say to ye in goin', and I want ye to take it away with ye, for it may help some of ye to aid some onfortunit man and to feel as happy as I feel to-night. It is this" — and here the old man paused a moment and looked with the face of an angel at his guests as they stood gazing at him; then he impressively said : —

"I've lived nigh on to eighty year, and my head be whitenin' with the comin' and goin' of the years I have lived, and the Book has long been in my cabin. I have kept many a Christmas alone and in company, both, but never afore have I knowed the raal meanin' of the day nor read the lesson of it aright. And this be the lesson that I have larned and the one I want ye all to take away with ye as ye go — that Christmas is a day of feastin' and givin' and laughin', but, above everythin' else, it is the day for forgivin' and forgittin'. Some of ye be young and may yer days be long on the 'arth, and some of yer

heads be as white as mine and yer years be not many, but be
that as it may, whether our Christmas days be many or few,
when the great day comes round let us remember in good or ill
fortun', alone or with many, that Christmas, above all else, is
the day for forgivin' and forgittin'."

The guests were gone and the Trapper seated himself in
front of the fireplace, and called the two dogs to his side. It
was a signal that they had heard many times and they responded with happy hearts. Each rested his muzzle on the
Trapper's knee, and fixed his large hazel, love-lighted eyes wist-
fully on his master's face. The old man placed a large and
age-wrinkled hand on either head, and murmured : "Whether
ye be in sorrer or joy, friends come and go, but, ontil death
enters kennel or cabin, the hunter and his hounds bide together.
The lad camps beyond sight and beyond hearin'. Henry be on
the other side of the world, to-night, and guests be gone.
Rover, yer muzzle be as gray as my head, and few be livin' of
the many we have met on the trail." And the Trapper lifted
his eyes and looked around the large and empty room, and
then added :—

"It took me a good many years, yis, it sartinly took me a
good many years, but, if I've larned the lesson of Christmas a
leetle late, I've larned it at last. But the cabin does look
a leetle empty now that the guests be gone. No, the lad can
never come back, and Henry is on the other side of the world,

THE OLD TRAPPER AND HIS DOGS.

" Friends come and go, but until death enters kennel or cabin, the hunter and his hounds bide together."

and there is no good in longin'. But I do wish I could jest tech the boy's hand."

Ah, friends, dear friends, as years go on and heads get gray —how fast the guests do go! Touch hands, touch hands with those that stay. Strong hands to weak, old hands to young, around the Christmas board, touch hands. The false forget, the foe forgive, for every guest will go and every fire burn low and cabin empty stand. Forget, forgive, for who may say that Christmas day may ever come to host or guest again. Touch hands.

W. H. H.—ADIRONDACK—MURRAY'S

COMPLETE
WORKS

CAREFULLY REVISED AND ENLARGED BY THE AUTHOR
PUBLISHED FOR THE FIRST TIME IN

UNIFORM EDITION

AND SOLD ONLY
BY SUBSCRIPTION
IN SETS OF FIVE
VOLUMES. . . . . .

ADIRONDACK TALES

PUBLISHED BY

ADIRONDACK PUBLICATION COMPANY

DO NOT FORGET

THAT MR. MURRAY'S
BOOKS ARE SOLD ...

ONLY BY SUBSCRIPTION,

AND CAN BE OBTAINED <u>ONLY</u>
FROM SOME AUTHORIZED AGENT,
OR DIRECTLY FROM THE AUTHOR

IN ALL MATTERS RELATING TO HIS WRITINGS
OR HIS PLATFORM ENGAGEMENTS, ADDRESS THE
. . . . . AUTHOR PERSONALLY . . . . . .

❧ ❧ ❧ ❧

ADDRESS,

W. H. H. MURRAY,
❧ GUILFORD, CONN. ❧
CARE THE MURRAY HOMESTEAD.

☞ *CANVASSERS WANTED IN EVERY CITY AND TOWN.*